GOBLINS!

You whip your stallion Stardark down the path. As you race round a bend, you see mounted goblins, brandishing weapons and shouting in glee. Frantically, you urge Stardark on, but then the horse stumbles, throwing you head over heels. As the terrified stallion bolts ahead, leaving you behind, a colorful figure somersaults over you, pulling a silver sword from his scabbard.

An elf! And he's attacking the goblins! Slaying two of the creatures sets the rest to flight. And, having rescued you, the elf now says, "You have two courses, lady fair. Seek your horse, or come with me to safety."

But can you trust an elf, even one this brave? And what about poor Stardark?

If you go with the elf, find your fate on Pathway 32 (page 124).

But if you search for Stardark, go to Pathway 45 (page 172).

Whichever choice you make, you will be exploring a new branch along your own private road to the Magic Realms. And no matter how your journey ends, when this adventure is finished, the fun will still go on. Just go back to the beginning of PLEDGE OF PERIL, and by making different choices, you'll discover a whole new series of exciting and challenge-packed DRAGONTALES adventures.

DRAGONTALES

Choose a Pathway to the Magic Realms

(0451)

#1☐ SWORD DAUGHTER'S QUEST by Rhondi Vilott. (130820—$1.95)*

#2☐ RUNESWORD! by Rhondi Vilott. (130839—$1.95)*

#3☐ CHALLENGE OF THE PEGASUS GRAIL by Rhondi Vilott. (130847—$1.95)*

#4☐ THE TOWERS OF REXOR by Rhondi Vilott. (130855—$1.95)*

#5☐ THE UNICORN CROWN by Rhondi Vilott. (132025—$2.25)*

#6☐ BLACK DRAGON'S CURSE by Rhondi Vilott. (132033—$2.25)*

#7☐ SPELLBOUND by Rhondi Vilott. (132858—$2.25)*

#8☐ THE DUNGEONS OF DREGNOR by Rhondi Vilott. (132866—$2.25)*

*Prices slightly higher in Canada

Buy them at your local bookstore or use this convenient coupon for ordering.

NEW AMERICAN LIBRARY,
P.O. Box 999, Bergenfield, New Jersey 07621

Please send me the books I have checked above. I am enclosing $_____
(please add $1.00 to this order to cover postage and handling). Send check
or money order—no cash or C.O.D.'s. Prices and numbers are subject to change
without notice.

Name_____

Address_____

City_____ State_____ Zip Code_____

Allow 4-6 weeks for delivery.
This offer is subject to withdrawal without notice.

DRAGONTALES #13

PLEDGE OF PERIL
by Rhondi Vilott

Illustrations by Freya Tanz

A SIGNET BOOK
NEW AMERICAN LIBRARY

NAL BOOKS ARE AVAILABLE AT QUANTITY DISCOUNTS WHEN USED TO PROMOTE PRODUCTS OR SERVICES. FOR INFORMATION PLEASE WRITE TO PREMIUM MARKETING DIVISION, NEW AMERICAN LIBRARY, 1633 BROADWAY, NEW YORK, NEW YORK 10019.

Copyright © 1985 by Rhondi Vilott Salsitz

Illustrations copyright © 1985 by Freya Tanz

Cover art by Tom Hallman

DRAGONTALES is a trademark of New American Library

All rights reserved.

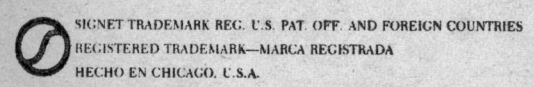

SIGNET TRADEMARK REG. U.S. PAT. OFF. AND FOREIGN COUNTRIES
REGISTERED TRADEMARK—MARCA REGISTRADA
HECHO EN CHICAGO, U.S.A.

SIGNET, SIGNET CLASSIC, MENTOR, PLUME, MERIDIAN and NAL BOOKS are published by New American Library,
1633 Broadway, New York, New York 10019

First Printing, June, 1985

1 2 3 4 5 6 7 8 9

PRINTED IN THE UNITED STATES OF AMERICA

With thanks to Shana and Sarah, for consenting to be heroines; and to my mother and my Maureen, with love

Stardark is the most beautiful horse in the world, and he belongs to you, Princess Sarah of the tiny valley kingdom of Marcelayne. You named him for the velvety darkness of the night sky between the twinkling stars, and his coat is the same jet black. There isn't a white hair on his head, not even in his soft muzzle and shining mane and tail. This fiery stallion has only known one rider—you—and that surprises you a little, but not when you remember how you raised him from hand when he was just a tiny foal and you were little older than your small sister Shana.

You're a princess through and through, with ribbons in your waist-long hair, and frocks that brush the ground as you walk, and you embroider with the best and know all the secrets of running the palace as smoothly as your mother, the queen. The only thing unladylike about you is the fiery steed Stardark. Any maybe that is why you love him so much, for he is wild and free

7

the way you can never be, for a royal princess has obligations.

With an inquisitive snort, the black stallion approaches the rail as you lean over it. He nuzzles your empty hands and peers at you from under his heavy forelock, brown eyes puzzled.

"You ate your sugar already, you greedy thing," you tease him. He nods his head up and down and lets out a gust of air. He paws the ground, eager to be away on your morning ride.

"Not today. I've invitations to do, menus to plan—we're giving a ball! Mother says it's time I met a prince."

The stallion continues looking at you, his proud neck arched. Even though he has the highest, largest pasture, he doesn't like being penned in. He lets out a whicker.

"It's not that I don't want to meet a prince," you tell him. "I really do! Dancing, my first kiss . . . my heart pounds when I think about it. But there're other things too . . . things no horse can understand. And it's not fair to you. Maybe Shana can start riding you—then you could still have your runs. I'm going to be awfully busy soon."

But the horse throws up his head disdainfully and kicks away from the fence, running wild and free across the sun-lit grass.

With a sigh, you turn away from the railing. You have music lessons, and then must sit with your mother and help her plan the state dinner that is only a few months away, to honor the allies of your kingdom and to try to make friends once more with the suspicious elves of the Dynas Mountains.

If only meeting with the proper princes weren't—weren't so businesslike. If only you could fall in love as Mother did, when your father first came to rescue her. If only . . .

As you walk down from the high pasture, you can see the smoke from the castle chimneys, dark and threatening. Odd. You smooth down the many skirts and petticoats of your dress as you approach the stableyard—and see the lads running helter-skelter, shouting and waving their hands at you.

"Run, princess! Run for it!"

Your heart pounds in fear, as you lift your skirt and prepare to bolt from the stable, for something is dreadfully, dreadfully wrong—and then a horrible ogre jumps in front of you, waving its spear!

"Stop, girl!" the beast commands, with a gnash of its tusks. You freeze in your steps.

You can hear the shrill sounds of dogs barking the alarm, and a faint scream in the morning air. The city gates are wide open, cracked like an egg! What has happened while you were at the pastures feeding Stardark his lumps of sugar?

More ogre soldiers surround you, and with a poke from a spear, you are herded to the castle, where you can see a sweaty and begrimed ogre army holding court in the yard. Invaded! Captured with barely a struggle, you can see, as the captain of the guard sits at the foot of his unit, his uniform torn, his weapons stripped from him.

Your father! And mother, and younger sister! What of them? Even as the ogre soldiers urge you forward, Shana bursts from the house, her feet flying, her dark hair wild about her intense face, eyes blazing from under her bangs.

"Run, Sarah, run!" she screams even as the soldiers bolt after her. They catch her up by the hem of her skirts, with a rip of fabric, and hold her dangling in the air.

You smile bravely at her. "I've already been caught, Shana," you say quietly. "Be quiet for a moment."

Shana kicks and twirls in midair, then clenches her fists. She glares at the ogre guard. "Put me down."

The ogre merely grunts.

You look at the terrible beast-man. "You have my word . . . Shana will stay with me."

"By all means, put girl down," a voice booms out of the great hallway leading to the throne room.

As Shana scrambles to her feet and clutches at your petticoats, a great hulk of an ogre strides to the doorway and stands with his mailed hands on his hips.

Rastik, the fearsome ogrelord of the wastelands! Longtime enemy of your father, defeated and exiled many years ago . . . before you were even born. Rastik, of some magic and much malice, gone so long that you all had forgotten he swore to come back someday. And now he has, so swiftly and surely that the kingdom of Marcelayne has fallen without a fight.

Shana tugs on your skirts. "He's got Mother and Father," she hisses.

"I know," you answer quietly, determined not

to let Rastik know your heart is pounding like a drum.

"I know how to get them free," your sister begins, but you shush her.

You lift your chin proudly. "Imprison us with the rest of my family," you demand of Rastik.

The brutish forehead wrinkles, and the dark eyes glare at you.

Shana tugs on you again. "I know . . ." she begins again, but Rastik beckons and the ogre soldiers drop their pikes threateningly at you, and the two of you are herded into the palace after the ogrelord.

Already, the beautiful tapestries and banners and paintings lining the halls have been stripped and trampled. Chairs are broken, and priceless inlaid tables smashed. You swallow your dismay at the sight of your beautiful home being destroyed by these beasts.

Your father and mother, shackled to each other, are sitting dejectedly at the foot of the throne.

King Joseph jumps to his feet as you enter the room. "Sarah! Are you all right?"

You nod, your throat tight with fear at the sight of them.

Shana whispers, "We hoped you'd gone riding . . . and escaped!"

If only you had! You could have brought help back from the Elash desert, perhaps. The nomads there have sworn allegiance to Marcelayne for countless decades.

Rastik bounds across the room to sit on the throne, his massive studded-leather bulk almost

11

dwarfing the chair. He laughs, and his cruel voice echoes throughout.

"You're done for now, Joseph! I've won!"

"Perhaps," your father answers. "And perhaps not. My kingdom encompasses many leagues, and you have only captured the heart of it."

"Yes, but cut out that heart," snarls the ogrelord with a clenched fist, "and the rest of many a beast will die!"

He's right. You go to your mother, who hugs you closely, as the ogre guards approach with shackles and chains for you and Shana.

Shana stomps her foot. "You big bully! I bet you couldn't win in a fair fight."

The orgelord raises a bristly eyebrow. "Indeed? I don't lose my bets."

You pull back on your little sister's skirts, but Shana is determined. She says to you, "I know his weakness!"

She darts in front of the throne. "Well, I know one you'd lose! I'll bet that my sister and her horse, Stardark, can win any race you name!"

The orgelord's face twitches. He is rolling something in one hand, and you see now it is dice. You remember that Shana has been here all morning, and her sharp eyes have seen a lot. Rastik must be a gambler.

Rastik leans forward, his beady eyes staring holes into you. "This pink spun-sugar princess in petticoats and ribbons win a horserace? That I have to see!"

"Bet the kingdom on it?"

The ogrelord and the little girl are nearly

brow to brow. Rastik growls, "I already have the kingdom."

King Joseph thunders, "Not surrendered, you don't. But if my daughter loses, I will order my men to lay down their arms."

All eyes are on you as chills slide down your spine.

"Do you have a fast horse?"

"The fastest," you say, surprised that your voice is not stuck in your throat.

Rastik sits back smugly, still rolling the dice in his hand. He waves Shana aside. "Do you know the Garden of Galatea?"

You nod. It's a long, long way away, perhaps a five-day trip, and it's a mystic garden. It's left strictly alone. There are supposed to be fabulous monsters guarding the rare herbs and flowers growing in it.

"Ride to the garden, pick me a black rose, and return in three days, before it wilts. If you can do this, I'll set your family and kingdom free. If not, it, and you, will be mine!"

Your mother gasps, and a hush falls over the throne room. But you stare at the ogrelord. Never will you be a bride to such a monster as this—or leave your family to his whims! You fall to your knee.

"I pledge to undertake this perilous journey! A rose within three days, or I agree to your terms!"

Rastik throws his head back, booming with laughter, as you rise. "Take her to the pastures! She has no time to waste!"

Shana is allowed to follow you out, as you pack

13

only water bags and a sack of dried jerky and berries. You haven't even time to change your dress. The ogre soldiers are already dragging Stardark down from the pasture.

The stallion is fighting their ropes, neighing and rearing in anger, as they drag him to the courtyard. His voice fairly trumpets his defiance, and Rastik watches keenly as you whistle down Stardark's fury and stroke him while the stablemaster bridles and saddles him for you. You can see the barest gleam of doubt on the ogrelord's face.

Shana kisses you.

"Which way will you go?" your sister whispers anxiously.

You shake your head. "I don't know!" An ogre guard tosses you into the saddle, and you gather the reins.

The townspeople have gathered fearfully to see you off. Rastik raises his fist and drops it. "Begone!" the monster thunders, and you set heels to Stardark and charge into the streets.

Cheers follow you as the wind catches your hair and you race through the city gates. Ogres pace you for a few leagues, their own mounts soon foaming and dropping behind the swift hoofbeats of Stardark.

At the edge of the city, you draw rein a moment.

There are three routes that will take you to the Garden of Galatea. The shortest is through the horrible swamps, the Manofee Hole, or the Swamps of Despairing, as your people refer to the bogs. They are treacherous beyond belief. The next route is directly through the Dynas Mountains, where

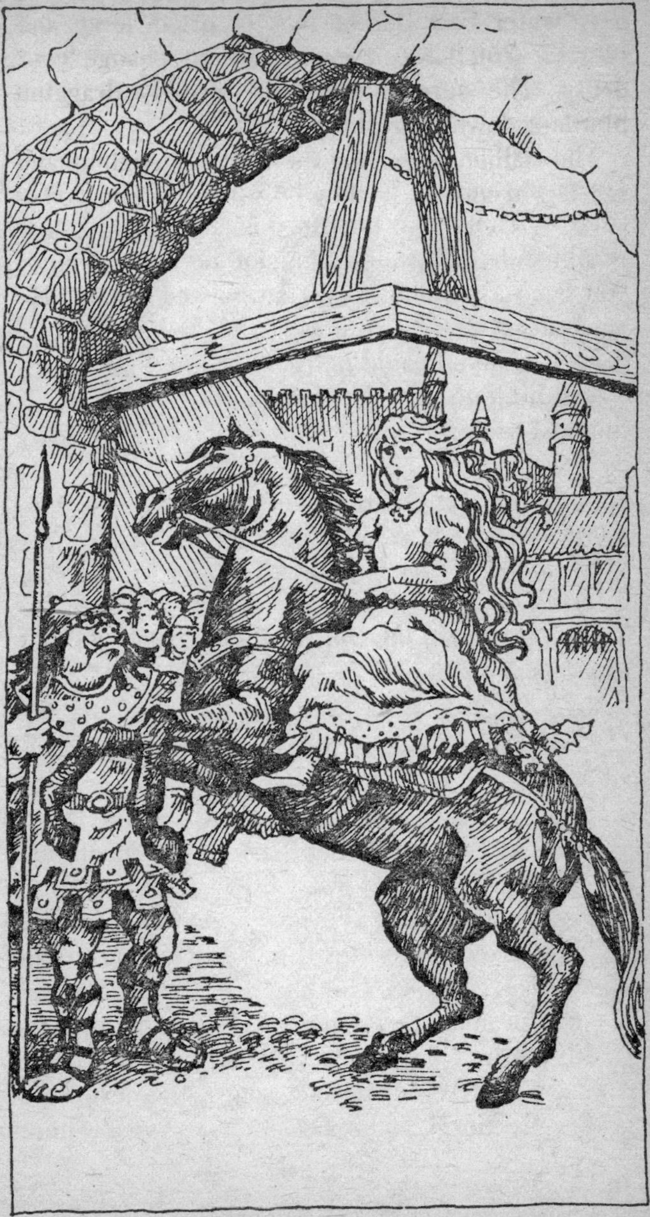

the elves reign—those same elves your father has long been trying to court as allies and whose heart and mind no one knows for sure. The longest, but probably safest, is across the Elash desert.

Stardark prances as you stroke his bowed neck. He is anxious to be on the open road, scarcely tired or damp from his run this far. You will have your hands full pacing him, for he doesn't know you have a grueling three days ahead of you. He has a heart only to race as fast as he can until he drops—and you could not bare to lose him!

You hesitate but a second longer. Which way is the best to go?

1. If you take the road to the desert, turn to Pathway 12 (page 53).
2. If you dare the Manofee Hole, go to Pathway 21 (page 88).
3. And if you try the Dynas Mountains, find Pathway 5 (page 29).

PATHWAY
1

You hesitate, then remember that Neal did rescue you from Old Man Willow. If he were a spy, he would have simply left you in that trap. Though you are wary, you nod.

Neal pulls you to your feet and then gathers up his fishing gear. He throws his boots into the nearly empty basket and then shoulders it with an apologetic laugh. "No fish yet today, but I'll have some for dinner, sure."

The thought of dinner reminds you that you've not yet had lunch . . . or breakfast, for that matter. Your stomach rumbles in an unseemly manner for a princess, and as Neal looks at you, the two of you break into laughter. He holds his hand up.

"I promise I'll stop soon, but the ogres have been by here once or twice, and we can't rest yet."

As he says that, he straps on a short sword, and your eyes widen, but you say nothing. It only confirms that Neal isn't exactly what he says he is.

As you turn back into the depths of the swamp,

he cuts a staff from a tree and skins it quickly to its milk-white wood. The limb is fragrant as he hands it to you. "A staff, if you can manage this and the reins."

"Thank you," you answer as you accept the walking stick.

"Don't thank me . . . you'll need it. Let the stick tell you if the ground is firm enough to step on, or if you see what appears to be a dead branch lying on the path, prod it before you step over. Many a snake has tricked its prey that way here." He turns away too quickly to see you shudder.

True to his word, the three of you stop and lunch in an hour. Stardark makes a meal of rush grasses and berries, while Neal has bread and cheese to add to your meager supplies. But his quick wit and easy way make the meal seem almost like a banquet, and your face is flushed when at last you break camp and travel on to the promised rose bush.

Neal has pulled on his own boots now and moves cautiously ahead of you. He signals for you to tie Stardark and join him, as he parts moss-covered branches and peers at a sapphire pool.

There, in the soft ground by the fresh water, grows a rose bush as lovely as any in the king's garden, and its flowers are a velvety black, like the coat of Stardark.

"It's there! It really is!" you gasp in delight, before Neal shushes you and pulls you back.

"What is it?"

"Fireflies, giant ones. They'll attack if you rouse them."

Even as he speaks, the dark swamp sky is suddenly lit up, as angry hums whiz over your head.

"Too late," mutters Neal. "They've spotted us." He pulls his short sword. "We'll have to fight if you want the rose."

1. *Will you fight the giant fireflies? If so, turn to Pathway 44 (page 168).*

2. *If you run from the angry hornetlike creatures to think of another plan, go to Pathway 13 (page 59).*

PATHWAY 2

"Run, Stardark," you cry softly, as you turn the horse in the tunnel and head him back the way you came.

Tyrone clicks his tongue in elfin impatience as the horse trots off, and you join him once again.

Too late, for the sword flares a bright white, and with hoarse cries, goblins jump at you from out of the darkness.

Their dank, sweaty bodies knock you aside, and you hear Tyrone give a muffled curse as his sword rings against stone. He battles as well as he can without the room to swing the blade properly.

You are picked up and slung over a wide, smelly, hairy shoulder, as Tyrone goes down with a cry, and the two of you are captured. The only good thing about it is that you are carried the length of the tunnel in the direction you were originally headed, until you are unceremoniously dumped on the stony ground.

Your head lands on Tyrone's shoulder, and he groans.

"Are you all right?"

There is a pause before the prince says, "Yes, I think so. I'm well tied—are you?"

Your hands are very well tied behind your back. "Yes. Have they gone?"

"Yes, all of them."

"Where?"

He straightens, so that you may, and soon you are sitting back to back. "They've gone to get their warlord. I suspect they'll come back, question us, and then roast us."

"Good."

Tyrone tenses as you answer, and then laughs as you let out a whistle.

"Think that horse will come, when he wouldn't budge earlier?"

"It's our only hope." You grow silent in the tunnel, trying to see where you cannot, only gray shadows against darker ones. You're very aware of the warmth of Tyrone's broad shoulders and the slower beating of his heart.

"I thought elves were cold," you say quietly.

He laughs, an ironic sound in the dark. "Some are. I would say, where you are concerned, I am quite . . . warm."

"You are?"

"Yes. You have captured an elfin heart, my mortal princess, though in this position there's nothing I can do about it."

"You can whistle, can't you?"

Another laugh, and then Tyrone's whistle joins yours.

After long moments, you hear the slow, hesitant clop of horse hooves on the tunnel floor. Shortly, Stardark is nuzzling you impatiently, pulling at your dress as you tease him with cries of "Apples! Apples!" Sharp teeth click away at your ropes, and you are free, even as Star snorts in disappointment that apples are nowhere to be found.

Tyrone leaps gaily to his feet. "This way, and quickly then, for there's no time to waste." And he leads you out of the tunnel and mountain in a matter of moments, for the goblins had taken you almost the rest of the way.

The two of you mount Stardark, after Tyrone soothes him with elfin words, and the stallion settles down. The valley of Galatea's Garden stretches in front of you.

Stardark slows to a walk as the wall of the Garden looms in front. Tyrone clucks in dismay and says, "The dragon's there, but it appears to be sleeping."

You slide out of the saddle, knowing that you can't take the horse any farther, and the elf jumps down lightly to join you.

"One of us will have to distract it, in case it awakens, and the other will have to fetch the—what is it? Ah, yes, the black rose."

"I'll get the rose."

"Ah, but Sarah—elves are as light as eiderdown."

"Then you get the rose."

"On the other hand, it is your quest."

You sigh.

1. Turn to Pathway 16 (page 69) if you go for the rose.

2. Go to Pathway 7 (page 42) if Tyrone goes for the rose.

PATHWAY 3

You shake your head. "It's dark now, and I have but two more days to finish my race. I have to return through the desert or the mountains, and it's too much to ask Stardark to carry two."

He scrubs a boot toe in the dust. "I understand," he says, in a low voice. "Well, then, goodbye, Princess Sarah, and good luck to you."

You touch your heel to Stardark and leave the boy behind.

The valley is farther than you thought, and you must stop in the groves, for it soon becomes too dark to ride. It's just as well, because your mount needs to rest, and the blades of green grass tempt him. As you climb off, your stiff and bruised muscles complain loudly. Maybe you shouldn't have left Neal behind after all—he still has herbed tea. With a giggle at that, you sink to the foot of a tree trunk and doze off into fitful sleep.

In the morning, you feel hot and flushed, and your chest and throat hurt terribly. You can hardly see Stardark to mount him, and you're too tired to do anything but sit in the saddle. As he takes hesitant steps without your sure hands on the reins, you doze off again, sick and fevered.

When you awaken, you're in your own silken bed, and your mother is leaning over you, with a cool cloth in her hand. She smiles, and the chains are gone from her slender wrists.

"Rest, Sarah."

"B-but . . . where am I?"

"Stardark brought you home. You've been very ill."

You lean back against the soft pillows. You ache all over. "What happened? Did I get the rose?"

Your mother laughs. "No rose. But you brought home a terrible fever from the swamp."

"No rose! Then I lost."

Shana pops up from the side of the bed, her dark bangs swinging. "No! You came home sick, and Rastik caught it and died, and some of the others got real sick, and they all got scared and left!"

"All because of me?" you ask weakly.

"That's right," your mother answers. "Now you get some rest! You've been ill."

And as you drift away, you slip into pleasant dreams.

THIS IS THE END OF YOUR ADVENTURE.

PATHWAY 4

"**G**o on! I can't quit. You must understand."

His solemn face watches you, as the red stallion stomps the ground. Then his eyes flicker to Stardark.

"He bears the weight, so the injury is minor, but you can't ride him farther. Ride with me—I know the way to the Garden of Galatea."

The nomad prince pulls you aboard his horse, saying, "Arrow can carry two for quite a way. Then, when we reach the Garden, who knows what will happen? It is said a wood nymph cares for the growing things, and a dragon prevents the nymph from escaping or giving out the miracles of what she grows."

"A dragon!" A cold arrow pierces your heart, then melts away. "No one said anything about a dragon."

Garon smiles. "That is a legend of my people. Who knows?" Then he kicks Arrow into a smooth lope, as he tightens an arm about your waist.

Stardark follows hesitantly, and your throat tightens as you can see the pain he is obviously in. You turn your face away so that Garon can't see your tears.

After many long leagues, you sense a change in the flat plains of the Elash. You are climbing a slope. You straighten in Garon's arms.

A shrill neighing breaks through, interrupting you as you speak.

"What is that?"

Garon reins his horse to a stop. The tired beast halts gratefully and lowers his head, breathing loudly.

The two of you look back. A herd of wild horses sweeps across the foot of the slope as Garon points.

"There is a well not far from here. The untamed have been drinking at it."

Stardark pauses at the foot of the slope too, his head held high, his ears pricked and nostrils flared. You can sense his pain and his pride, and his eagerness to join the untamed.

Garon says softly, "He may never be able to bear your weight again . . . but he will heal enough to run free."

Your heart feels as though it's in your throat. You know that Garon will carry you back to Marcelayne—that you can borrow another desert horse if need be—but what can you do about Stardark?

He burns to run free.

1. Will you set him loose? If this is your wish turn to Pathway 23 (page 95).

2. Go to Pathway 43 (page 163) if you keep him and take him with you to the Garden.

PATHWAY 5

"Mountains it is," you decide with a sigh, looking at the road that leads into the Dynas Mountains, land of tall, purple spires, chill winds, and treacherous elves. Not that the elves were always treacherous, no—but they are so much longer-lived than men that they ofttimes regard the affairs of men as unimportant, and pay little attention, as your father would say.

Well, this moment may be but a sneeze to them, but it's the most important thing that's ever happened in your life. You knee Stardark, turning the impatient stallion onto the steeply winding path.

By the time you have long left the lands of your kingdom, you have torn off one of your petticoats and fastened it about your neck and shoulders for warmth, caring little about how ridiculous you look—you're cold! Though winter is officially gone and spring just begun, the breeze howling down through the Dynas Mountains talks of eternal snows and land that is never free of ice. How could anyone live up here and be happy?

You rein Stardark to a halt, and he swishes his tail. You are mountain-high, and the craggy rocks about you are broken only for the pathway, and by an occasional pine tree. Water trickles down through the granite, speaking of underground streams and snow pockets, water strong enough to seep through rock. You take a deep breath, and your ears pop. You shiver. There's no way you can spend a night up here unless you and Stardark keep moving.

At that, you kick him forward, as pebbles tumble down from the jagged peak above and scatter at your heels. Something is above you, and Stardark nickers as a growling echoes about you. You look up, and see a goblin face and a triangular wolfish face, green eyes aglow, and then the face disappears.

Goblins! Riding on worgs, those huge wolfish animals bred for their use! You whip Stardark down the path, and the horse agrees, nodding his head in time to his ever-lengthening strides.

As you clatter around a bend in the pass, you can see the worgs leaping to the ground behind you, goblins shouting in glee, brandishing weapons and shields. Your heart in your throat from terror, you frantically urge Stardark ahead, for goblins are known to love both horse and human flesh. Though the stallion runs as fast as he can over the broken, unfamiliar ground, his breath rattles in his lungs, and the wolfish animals gain ground, their goblin masters beating their ribs with their horny feet.

The pass opens up, flat ground, and you lean low over Stardark's neck. Then he stumbles, and you are thrown, tumbling head over heels. A tuft

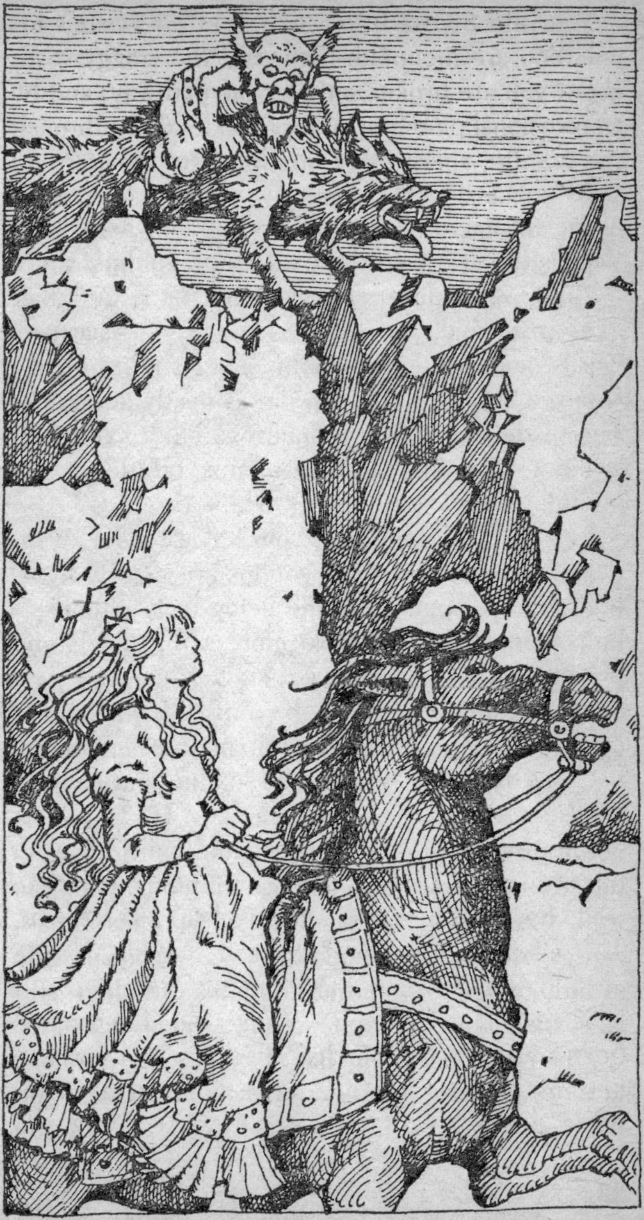

of grass breaks your fall, and you lie panting, as a colorful figure somersaults over your head, shouting foreign words, and pulling a silver sword from his scabbard.

Bit in his mouth, lips foamed in terror, Stardark bolts down the path, and you are left to the mercy of the strange being as he calls out a challenge and slashes the sword in the path of the goblins.

Tall and slender, with pointed ears, and hair like spun gold, the elf prince calls out haughty words, and as the first goblin charges past him, he cuts the goblin from the worg as neatly as can be. The blade sparks as it touches worghide, and with a howl of pain, the beast runs off down the mountainside.

You crawl to your feet, your ankle tender, wondering if the elf and the goblins are merely fighting over the spoils or if the being truly intends to help you. You wonder no more as he pivots and points sword blade at you.

"Stay behind me. I'll be finished with these cowards in a minute." He scarcely finishes before hacking the head off a second goblin, and another riderless worg chases after the first.

The third goblin, elbows flapping, pulls his worg out of sword reach and goes gallumphing down the trail, howling curses with every leap of his beast. The elf prince laughs, long and heartily, before cleaning his sword and sheathing it carefully.

Then he looks at you. "Well, well. Long has it been since I visited the halls of men—is it now the custom to wear your undergarments about your neck?"

You feel your face hot with embarrassment, even as you fold your arms about your chest, both shivering with cold and trying to hide the petticoat. When you find your tongue, you only say, "Thank you for saving me. And now I will be off to find my horse."

The elf prince leaps to bar your way, bowing with a flourish of his long sleeves, his blond hair parting about his upswept and pointed ears. "Please . . . don't be offended. We elves have a prankish humor. Surely you've heard that. I be Tyrone. And who might you be?"

You're aware that your hem is torn, your dress dirty, your petticoat about your neck, your ribbons long since flown from your tangled hair, and this idiot wants to know who you are with a courtly bow. You sigh. "I'm Sarah. Sarah of Marcelayne, daughter of King Joseph."

His clothes of gold and sky blue seem to ripple with movement, though Tyrone stands still in front of you. He looks into your eyes, and for a second, it's as though he swept you off your feet and carried you with him, whirling, through a dance of centuries. Then he smiles gently and takes your elbow, for you are feeling faint, and he says, "Of course. Not *that* Joseph. You must mean Joseph the Younger, who ran off that ogre scoundrel Rastik."

Released from the spell of his eyes, you stammer, "Th-that's him. And Rastik is back, and has taken my family hostage. I am . . . trying to free them." Your mind whirls at the thought that this young elf prince, who appears little older than you, refers to your great-grandfather, a warrior who led armies against elves in centuries past.

"Well now. You have two courses, lady fair. To seek your horse, or to come with me and see what must be done about Rastik."

He presents an arm, with a mocking smile and bow, and you remember the many warnings of your youth not to ride in the Dynas Mountains, for your father had no treaty with the elves and they are regarded as tricky creatures.

Nor do you feel right about Stardark, with worgs on the loose and possibly trailing him. At the very least he could step on a loose rein and stumble again.

1. If you go with the elf, find your fate in Pathway 32 (page 126).

2. But if you search for your horse, go to Pathway 45 (page 174).

PATHWAY
6

"It's a hard thing I ask, but you must know also that I don't ask for my kingdom alone. Under Rastik's cruel leadership, there will be no freedom for us, or water for you. Please come back with me and help set my father free!"

The tall nomad bows his head in thought. There is a dead silence over the camp, for even the playing children are quiet. One heartbeat, two, then three and four. Finally, on the tenth heartbeat, he raises his head. "It will be done," he answers quietly. "Send the call out by drummer to gather the tribes."

Garon surges to his feet, punching his fist into the air in excitement. "War!"

His people jump up also, crying strange words, their faces flushed with excitement, though you sit, huddled, fearful that you have asked them to do a terrible and disastrous thing.

In the morning, you stretch and wake, blinking in wonderment, then realize you are sleeping underneath a wagon. The sounds of people hurrying back and forth, horses whickering in eagerness, the sounds of their harnesses clicking and creaking awaken you fully. This morning the nomad tribes will have gathered in strength, the drum messages having thrummed through most of the night.

You roll out from under, just as Garon pauses by the wagon and leans down to look at you. You bump noses as you stand, and, embarrassed, you duck your head away as Garon laughs heartily.

"Sleepyhead! We are close to leaving without you."

As you look around, you gasp, for you are surrounded by hundreds of warriors, in hard leather armor, and half-helms, winged and horned, silken banners and flashing weapons. They look barbaric and dreadful, and even eager to fight! Their blue-black hair is tied back with leather thongs, braided and contained by their leather headgear. Bared arms carry shields, carved from the precious wood of the Elash plains trees.

But the horses! Glorious and snorting, every color of the rainbow, grays, chestnuts, bays, blacks, paints, some gold as honey, they toss their long manes and tails and stamp the ground. Even so grand a horse as Stardark looks ordinary, for all the desert horses are sculpted from the same mold.

As if reading your thoughts, a loud trumpeting calls you from the milling band of warriors, and a black horse rears, tearing loose his reins from the hand of the nomad who holds him, and a black flash gallops across the dried plains grasses and plunges snorting to a halt in front of you, dropping his soft muzzle to your outstretched hand.

Garon laughs at the spectacle. "He shows off his mettle for you!"

You laugh, too. "I think he's a little jealous . . . he's never had any competition before."

A shield and tabard rattle from the saddle, and Garon unhooks them and presents them to you.

He helps you fasten the tabard over your sadly wilted pink dress, and his hands linger for a moment in your thick hair, lifting it out of the way as you settle the leathern gear about your chest. The feeling of his fingers at the back of your neck as he gently combs out a tangle sends goosebumps all over you.

As suddenly, he drops your hair and strides away, then stops and spins around. "My father and I will do our best for you, Princess Sarah, but use the shield well, for the ogres are excellent archers. Keep safe!"

You watch him walk away and mount his gray mare in a graceful vault, your heart pounding as a strange fever lights your cheeks. What are you feeling? With confused thoughts, you make Stardark kneel so that you can put your foot to stirrup and swing up.

The ride to Marcelayne is filled with the voices of the Elash nomads, singing chants and bold songs of daring deeds. Many women have joined their men, outfitted just the same, except that they have bows upon their backs and do not carry swords. One of them, an older woman with sad, dark eyes, rides closely by you.

"Why don't you carry a sword, too?" you ask

shyly as the army breaks in midday at a watering well.

She smiles as she stretches. "We do not fight in the front line, lest we be taken hostage, and so tear the fighting heart out of our men. We are the main archers of the force, and stay an arrow's flight away from the true battle."

"Oh." Her words strike home to you the battle ahead, the terrors of which have been obscured by the glorious singing. You remember that many may die because you have asked them to. Your breath is tight in your lungs, and you fight for a deep sigh.

She pats your arm. "Don't worry. Prince Garon and the king know what they are doing. Even if you had not asked and ridden your way, they would have ridden out, I think. Rastik's coming threatens all of us." Then she smiles, and little crow's feet deepen about her eyes. "And also, I think the king desires a marriage between your country and mine."

At that, she turns her horse and leads it to its turn at the well, leaving you once more with whirling emotions you barely understand.

By late afternoon, the Elash army has crossed the ridges and come up behind your city, and you rein up to overlook the captured town. Shunning the main road, the army has cut across the plains and desert and taken a little-known mountain pass, arriving hours before you thought you could, and with relatively fresh animals. You swallow, thinking that if your father had known the Elash could so appear out of nowhere, he might not have been so quick to trust them . . . but then, it makes you aware that this alliance is built on honesty and not fear.

Stardark snorts gently. Garon appears out of the masses at your side, silently, with a grim smile.

"We have dispatched two outpost guards, and are ready to start the attack. Stay with the archers, and mind that shield!"

You nod, your mouth dry, but as he reins away, you manage to call out, "Be careful . . . please."

His solemn eyes drill into yours, and you feel that strange fever rushing through your body again. A bold smile replaces the solemn look, and he whoops as he turns away, and gallops into the crowd, scattering warriors right and left. You bite your lip, happy that he cares that you care.

The single whoop turns into a roar, as the Elash surge down from the hills, shields raised, arrows nocked, swords unsheathed, and the broken ranks of Rastik's men scramble to meet the attack.

The air is filled with the thunder of the horses, the clash and clatter of weapons and shields, and above all, voices calling harsh words. You can hear Garon's voice, young and strong and a little higher than the other's, sounding out, "Breach the walls! Breach the walls!"

Time hangs heavy as Stardark dances nervously beneath you, and maids on either side let out the whoosh of arrows, nock, draw, and let flight again, their arching flight a thing of deadly beauty. Then all is silent, and you see the wave of Elash horsemen turning back.

"What's happened? What is it?" you cry out, misunderstanding the retreat.

Garon kicks and knees his mare through the crowd to you, his long face knotted in a frown. "The ogres have withdrawn successfully, before we could cut them down. Now we must lay siege."

Your heart sinks as the nomads dismount and draw into small clusters. The fields below you are littered with bodies, and yet the bulk of the ogre soldiers got away, and are now behind the stronghold of your father's city.

Eruman, the leader and Garon's father, approaches solemnly. "My humble apologies, Princess Sarah. We had hoped to succeed by surprise. I must now ask you what you know of your father's defenses."

Discouraged, you answer in a low voice. "The city is well provided for, and guarded, and we have three main wells. It will be difficult to starve us out, and the defenses are equally tough."

Stardark snorts as Eruman puts his rough, calloused hand on your knee. You look at the tall nomad, aware that gray peppers the blue-black hair at the temples, where a few strands have escaped the raven-winged helm he wears.

Garon blurts out, "Wait! You must have a secret passage that runs out of the castle, for escape. Every fort has one. Surely yours does."

"Why . . . yes." You hadn't thought of that before. Your own family would have used it had not Rastik shackled them and kept them under guard. You shudder. It's dusty and full of spiders and rats but then . . .

Eruman interrupts, "No, Garon. It's too risky. I won't allow it. A few cannot stand against the ogrelord. Remember his magic!" He turns to you. "With your permission, princess, we will launch a main attack. I ask your permission because your family is in danger if we do . . . but it may be their only hope."

The grinding and rolling of a massive catapult underscores his words. You look at the war machine, realizing the impact of his words. You swallow tightly.

"No, don't do that," Garon argues. "I know we can sneak in successfully."

The two look at you, father and son, awaiting for you to speak your will, but are you strong enough to make a decision? Should you guide Garon through the underground passage, which may or may not have been found by Rastik, or ask Eruman to start an all-out war against your once fair kingdom?

1. *If you agree to guide Garon in secrecy, turn to Pathway 18 (page 76).*

2. *Your fate lies in Pathway 46 (page 182) if you give your approval to Eruman's plan to attack the city.*

PATHWAY 7

You throw your arms about Tyrone's neck and kiss him. He smiles. "I'll get the rose," he says, and before you can say another word, he unclasps your arms and jumps to the garden wall.

Light as his promise, he flits across the stones and leaps into the branches of the rose tree, plucking a black rosebud and holding it aloft triumphantly.

The dragon stirs in its sleep, but doesn't notice as an elf prince painstakingly extricates himself from several thorns, jumps down, and races across the garden.

You are trying not to laugh as Tyrone vaults the wall and presents the rose to you. His fine coat is torn in several places.

"Next time," you whisper, "remember there are thorns."

He nods. "Right."

The two of you lead Stardark away, and then mount, heading for home. Part of Tyrone's magic makes the burden lighter than it would be, and Stardark's gait covers the leagues quickly, until you are cresting the road to home almost before you can realize it.

You awaken in Tyrone's arms as he says, "There it is."

You can see the town ahead of you, gates open, and it is dawn, dawn of the third day.

Tyrone slides off and takes your hand solemnly: "I can go no farther than this, Sarah, for this is the boundary of my land, too. Unless you wish me to go all the way home with you, and realize the consequences of that wish."

You look at his face, with pointed ears, and hair like spun gold, and eyes of deepest aquamarine. He is both old and young at the same time, and he is afraid to meet your gaze now.

"And if I should ask you, does this mean that there might be something more between us?"

Tyrone straightens, one hand toying with the hilt of his sword before he answers. He looks back to you. "Yes," he says quietly. "It is not unknown for one of my kind to meet and marry one of your kind. And if you ask me back with you, I would ask only that you consider me among your suitors."

Your heart beats loudly. Will you ask him or not?

1. *If you ask Tyrone to come with you to Marcelayne, turn to Pathway 9 (page 46).*

2. *But if you refuse his wish, go on to Pathway 22 (page 94).*

PATHWAY 8

Being sensible, you crawl back down the slope, knowing that three ogre soldiers are too much for you. Stardark nuzzles you tiredly as you gather his reins and lead him to a rock so that you can mount more easily.

The afternoon wears on as you let your tired horse pick his way through the sand and brush, and your hair hangs limply over your shoulders, and every step kicks up a cloud of dust that seems to go right to your throat. Even the little rock dogs, as you call them, fail to pop their heads out to look at you, the sun beats down so hotly.

How can even the nomads live here? But as you mop your damp forehead, you know that the great plains lie beyond here, and though they are still hot, the grass grows thickly and trees dot the landscape. It is called the Elash desert, but not all of the region is rightly named.

Stardark stumbles to a halt, and you rock in the saddle. *This* part is certainly desert. The sun shimmers off the ground, dazzling your eyes. As you shade them, you let out a tiny gasp of hope. The oasis! So close you can almost smell the water!

"There it is!" you cry joyfully, and you urge the black stallion into movement again, his tired strides eating up the ground. Like a dark bolt, the two of you dart into the oasis, its shadowed image welcoming you.

Whoosh! Ropes snake up about you, and an immense net rises about you, and a bell clangs madly as Stardark snorts and bucks, tangling the two of you even further. You fight for control of him, and calm him down to a trembling, snorting handful beneath you, and stroke his bowed neck.

This is no oasis! A mirage . . . you've traveled leagues out of your way into a mirage! And the ogre soldiers have beaten you here, and you've stumbled right into their nets.

Trapped. Snared like any rabbit. You sigh. The soldiers will no doubt come for you, if the desert lions don't find you first.

Right now, it looks as if Rastik has won another bet.

IS THIS THE END?

PATHWAY 9

Eagerly, you reach down for him. "Oh, yes! Come with me!"

With a shout of glee, the elf jumps back onto the horse behind you, his arms embracing you tightly as you ride down into Marcelayne.

He unsheathes his elfin blade, and the ogre soldiers give you clear passage as you ride to the castle, where cries of joy from the townspeople bring Rastik grumbling into the courtyard.

The ogrelord's beady eyes widen greatly as he spies you and the elf prince, and he cowers, much afraid of the magic blade. You hand him the rose triumphantly.

"I have run the race, and won! Leave now, Rastik!"

The beastly being does so, as Shana breaks out of the palace, joined by your mother and father.

Your little sister cries out in wonder.

"Look what Sarah brought home! An elf!"

And you all laugh, as Tyrone blushes a little and stops waving his sword about.

THE END

PATHWAY 10

You shake your head. "I made a pledge to run a race, and my word is my honor."

The nomads look at you through the smoky campfire. The leader clears his throat. "I, Eruman, hear you, and understand your words."

"Well, I don't," Garon blurts out, "Rastik has no honor!" And the boy stands up and swiftly strides away into the night.

Eruman sighs. "He is right, princess, but you must do what you can. Your horse will be ready in the morning."

In the morning light, you uncurl from a strange campfire, tired still and dirty from your night's rest. Stardark is hobbled near you, and he puts his muzzle down to your hair and blows softly.

"Yes, I'm awake," you mutter. Then your eyes open wide as you spy Garon standing by the stallion, his body tense.

He thrusts a small pouch into your hand. "Remember—whether the race is won or not, Rastik has little honor. This pouch is full of the sleeping poison. Feed it to him if he crosses you."

You scramble to your feet, but the nomad prince is gone, his form lost among the milling horse herds.

Hands trembling, you tuck the pouch into the front of your dress. The sleeping poison is a slow death that causes the victim to fall into sleeping fits, each longer than the last, until eventually the victim never awakens. The only good thing about the poison, if a poison can be said to be good, is that it is remedied fairly easily and the victim suffers no side effects. But you could never do such a thing!

There are fresh saddlebags hanging from Stardark's back, and he is ready to go. You unhitch the hobbles and look around, but it appears there will be no formal goodbye. You are on your own, as much as you were yesterday when you first started out.

You swing into the saddle, with a small cry, as your bruised legs let you know how stiff you are. A tiny scroll is tied to the reins, and you open it. A smile breaks across your face as you read a tiny map, and a dotted red line shows you a shortcut across the Elash desert.

No one answers your hail of farewell and thanks, save for a few small children who run with you to the edge of the camp and stand in the wagons' shadow as you and Stardark gallop away.

Time pounds at you now, for you must reach the Garden of Galatea by high noon this day or you will never make it back by tomorrow eve to win your bet. But Stardark strides out, strong and powerful, his body hugging the ground, as he runs for the sheer joy of it.

You run with him, holding tight to reins and mane, your own body feeling the exhilaration of the horse's power and beauty. Leagues fall away behind you. Then suddenly Stardark stumbles!

With a scream, you are hurtling through the air. The ground meets you with a *thud!* and an *oof!* and the wind is knocked from you. You roll on the dried grass, gasping for breath, and as soon as you have gained it, you crawl to Stardark and grab the reins.

The horse takes a step and then another, and you catch your breath, your heart stuck in your throat. Lamed! The stallion whickers and nuzzles his right foreleg, and as you run a hand over it, you can already feel the heat and swelling.

Lamed! Hot tears sting your face. Short of breaking his neck, you can't think of anything more disastrous. There is nothing to do but go home now, in total defeat, and become the ogrelord's unwilling bride.

The stallion lifts his muzzle and whuffles at you, as you cannot control your sobbing. You rub his jaw and scratch his favorite place, aware that he must be in terrible pain.

Stardark suddenly moves his head from your hands, ears pricked in alertness, but you pay no attention to him.

"There's nothing else to do now but go home," you say.

"That, or go on!" a strong young voice cries out, as you whirl in surprise. Garon sits atop his chestnut stallion, the one that matched strides in yesterday's race ahead of the ogre soldiers. His dark eyes blaze a challenge at you.

1. *Will you go home? If so, turn to Pathway 40 (page 153).*
2. *Or will you go on? Find Pathway 4 (page 26).*

PATHWAY
11

"**N**onsense! I won't leave him behind for anything. Here, quickly, help me push this old log into the water!"

You grab the stump of an old rotting log at the pool's edge, and together, the two of you push it in, the jagged end sinking right in front of Stardark. The horse snorts, seeming to realize what you are doing. He manages to free his front hooves and buck free of the pool, trampling the log to splinters under his heavy frame, and it is the log that is sucked down, not the horse, as the stallion scrambles out.

He shakes himself and stands, sides heaving, as you throw your arms about your neck.

Neal looks shamefaced at the ground. "I'm sorry. I was wrong," he murmurs.

"No, you were right about my obligations. It's just that I—I couldn't leave him behind to die like that!" You nudge Neal. "Come on—the ogre soldiers can't be far behind."

Quickly, the fisherboy heads through the swamp,

51

and the tangles of the branches whip in your face and slash at your hands, and pull at Stardark's reins, but you don't care, for you nearly lost your fabulous horse, and your heart with him.

At the swamp's edge, Neal hesitates, then points across the expanse, where you can see the river flowing from the mountains, with a green grove and valley at its foot.

"There . . . the place you seek is there." He pauses, as though unsure what to say, then blurts out, "Let me go with you."

You mount up Stardark and look down. He has been a help, there's no doubt of that, but what can a fisherboy do to help you further? Stardark would have to carry double, and that would slow him down and tire him even more. And you are, after all, a princess.

You hesitate as you look at the handsome youth and see the expression on his face. Why, you think, he might be in love with me. You turn away, embarrassed.

1. *If you take Neal with you, go to Pathway 33 (page 128).*

2. *Find your answer in Pathway 3 (page 24) if you leave Neal behind.*

PATHWAY
12

The Elash desert, you decide with a flip of the reins. More than a safe journey lies that way—perhaps allies you can rally against Rastik's invasion!

Stardark paws the ground and starts trotting toward the sere dry hills that mark the edge of the boundary between fair, green Marcelayne and the plains and deserts that the nomad tribesmen travel. His nostrils flare, and he shakes his head, mane cascading over his neck and reins, as though he can already scent the herds of rival desert stallions.

The lush green of your kingdom gives way to the wheel-rutted, dry-packed road leading across the rounded hills and toward the Elash. The grasses here have turned the color of wheat. You keep Stardark at a slow pace, saving his speed and endurance for the days ahead, picking the center of the road, fearful of the stallion's turning a fragile ankle in the deep wagon grooves made by caravaners.

As you near the top of the knolls, the hot dry wind off the desert strikes you, lifting your heavy hair off your shoulders and drying the lather on Stardark's neck. You haven't forgotten that it is because of the same wind that rainclouds coming off the mountain ranges drop their precious gift of water into the green valleys of your home, as they are unable to pass lightly across the desert unless storm-driven. If it were not for that, as told you many times by your parents, Elash would be the green and fertile plains and Marcelayne perhaps the desert!

It is because of this that water is never refused to the nomads. When their desert and plains wells go dry, they journey over the hills on foot, by horse and by wagon, a silent, dark-eyed people, dressed in bright silks and skins, their horses ridden wild with but a single tether for a rein. You can only remember once in your life when the nomads came for water, but that memory blazes in your mind. It was they who left Stardark behind, a colt without a mother, doomed to die if he was returned to a desert baking in drought. You raised him by hand and earned his undying love and loyalty. He is a fierce thing that sometimes makes you feel like an eagle riding the wind.

Stardark whickers as you draw rein on the knolls and cast a last glance back toward the valleys of your kingdom, thinking of the three days you have to save it.

Shadows cross your line of vision, and you freeze in your saddle. Riders, three dark riders, coming down the road, pausing only to check tracks. Suddenly, one of them spots you on the ridge and straightens in the saddle to point.

Ogre soldiers! You chew on your lip. You should have known Rastik wouldn't leave your racing to chance. Are they tracking you to stop you?

"They'll never catch us!" you cry out angrily, and you brace your feet in the stirrups. You flip the end of the reins down on Stardark's rump with a *pop!* The stallion snorts with eagerness as he breaks into a run. The dust flies from his hooves as you lean over his neck, wrapping your hands tightly in his thick mane. Let them try to catch you now!

Over the ridge and down into the desert, into its rocks and gullies, the two of you race. Soon the wind will cover your tracks and not even the ogre soldiers will be able to spot you, for the Elash is not a smooth, sandy desert, but a wilderness of boulders and hills, ravines and shrubberies.

You give Stardark his head, and he picks his way over the rough ground, slowing only a little to find a way to go, leaving the trading road behind. You will return to it when the ogre soldiers have been left behind.

You finally slow Stardark down, the stallion fighting the bit and then giving in, his neck shiny with his effort, as he clambers out of a gully and pauses on a hard-baked surface. The clay beneath you is seamed and cracked, like an earthenware spiderweb.

Your pink frock is covered with dust, and you shake it out as the silence of the Elash washes over you. Only Stardark's heavy breathing can be heard. You let him rest a moment until you can refresh him with water from the bags slung behind the saddle.

A tiny sound behind you makes you twist in the

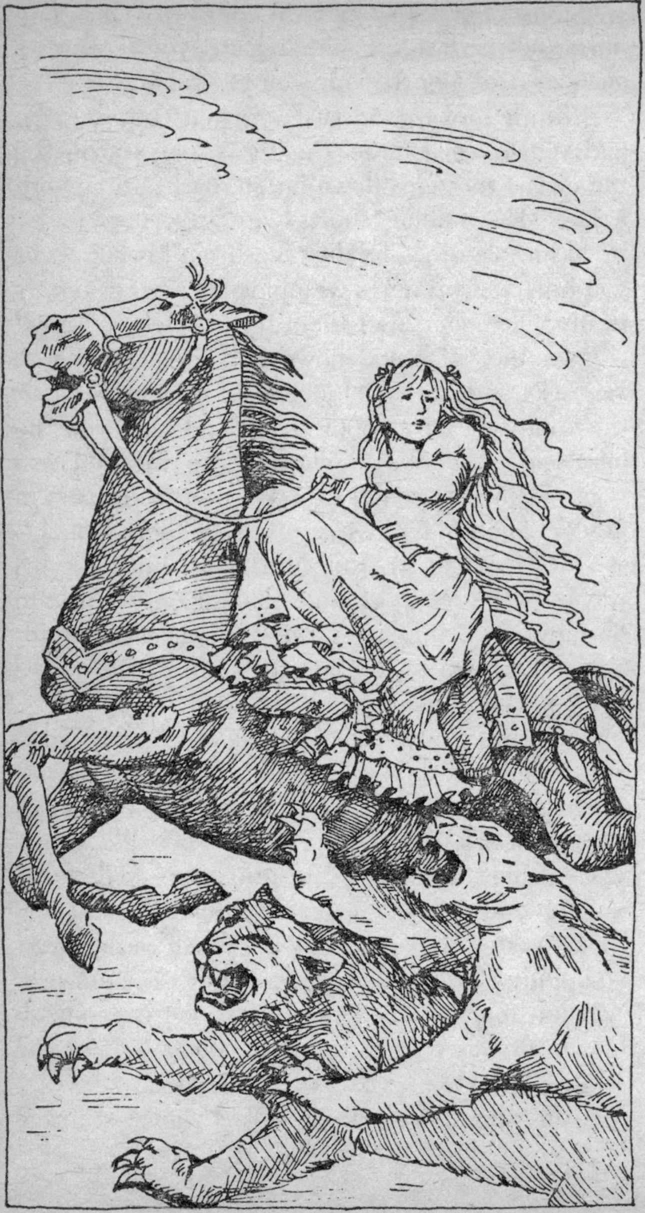

saddle—and you scream! White fangs and gleaming yellow eyes, tousled manes and tufted tails flick as one, as two desert lions stalk you quietly, crawling forward on their lean and hungry bellies.

With a roar, the tawny beasts spring at you. Stardark bolts, and you grab for the saddle desperately, half on and half off.

The first beast fails in his leap and falls to one side, but the second desert lion snarls and spits. His claws rake across the pack and the hem of your dress with a horrible sound. His hot breath gusts in your face as his slanted eyes meet yours with a terrible hunger. The dress rips apart as you struggle to sit up, and the leather pack falls to the ground, the lion still entangled in it.

With snarls and roars, the lions bound after you as you kick Stardark, crying desperately for more speed from his tired limbs. Their hot breath seems to graze your back as they yowl in anger, and Stardark shows them his heels, leaving them growling in the desert.

Shuddering, you let Stardark run far, as you realize how close you came to the end. Stupid of you to forget that the desert has other perils besides the lack of water.

Finally, Stardark draws to a halt, head lowered, white foam flecking his neck and shoulders. You see with a troubled heart that both water bags as well as your supplies have been ripped away.

You can't go far without water. You look back over the ground, seeing the clear track of your horse's hooves, and know that going back to retrieve your supplies is a definite option, for surely the lions will have mauled the food bag and then left, stalking other game.

Or you could strike out for the trading road, hoping to find an oasis or desert well, for you know the road across the Elash follows water.

You look at your torn petticoats and dusty slippers. Your hair is a hot and dirty tangle, and the sun is dotting your face with sweat. How thirsty Stardark must be after his running! You have to have water for drinking, and soon. Stardark gives a hefty sigh and turns his head to look back at you, as though he is wondering what you will do.

Time is wasting. What will you decide?

1. If you return to find your lost supplies, hoping the lions have gone, find Pathway 19 (page 82).

2. But if you go on, turn to Pathway 30 (page 120).

PATHWAY 13

You let out a scream as a firefly darts at your face, its heat and brilliance blinding you. You turn and run, and Neal has no choice but to follow you. The two of you stumble through the grove and swamps as Stardark plunges after you.

Finally you stop, panting. You look at Neal. "I'm sorry," you say, your voice quavering. "But that was too much. I'm just not cut out for all of this."

Neal sighs. "I understand, princess, but now we've a problem."

You squeeze out the hem of your dress, newly sogged. "And that is?"

"You're lost."

A cold chill runs through you as you look about and see nothing but desolate gray-green. You feel an incredible coldness about you, and Stardark raises his head and screams in terror, eyes rolling in his head, and you turn about to clutch at Neal for comfort.

And scream yourself, for it is not Neal standing

there, but a ghoul in Neal's clothes, a horrible being that smiles as it clutches for you.

"Lost forever in the swamps," it says in a hollow, whistling voice. "Lost as I was. The black rose is death, death, death. . . ."

THE END

PATHWAY 14

"It's the dark that frightens him," you argue, "but he'll come if I blindfold him." You rip off the hem of your newly repaired dress and reach up to wrap it about the horse's eyes. With a snort, Stardark puts his muzzle trustingly in your hands, and he steps forward as you pull him along.

For long hours, the two of you guide the reluctant horse through the maze of tunnels. Once, Tyrone freezes and flattens you against the wall, as the blade of his sword flares out, a silver light in the dark, but nothing happens, and the light fades, and then the prince breathes easier.

You must be nearing the end, you think, when a rock clatters and Tyrone drops your hand, his sword flaring white-hot, so suddenly in the dark you're nearly blinded.

He thrusts a stick into your hand. "Run for it! When you get clear of me, say, 'Evocare,' and the stick will become a burning torch. Take the horse and run!"

Saying this, he shoves you in front of him, as

goblin war cries ring out, and Tyrone is attacked on three sides. You break into a run, dragging Stardark behind you, the animal trotting blindly until you are far enough to cry the word Tyrone told you, and the stick catches fire.

You pull the blindfold from Stardark, and the two of you race through the tunnel, the ring and clang of battle following you until its thin echo fades out, and you realize your face is wet with tears, for you don't know if Tyrone lives or dies.

You burst suddenly into the open, at the foot of the mountain. You throw yourself on Stardark as you drop the torch into the dirt, and you kick him into a run, panic-stricken that you might have been followed. The black stallion doesn't falter until the leagues have passed under his hooves and his wide-cupped nostrils are wine-red. Shuddering, you rein him in, and see the stone-walled garden in front of you.

An emerald shadow stretches in front of you, stretches and preens, and unfurls wings, until a dragon blocks your entrance to the Garden of Galatea.

"Welcome, young maid. Welcome to the Garden of Galatea, where all manner of delights await you."

You are tired and weary and frightened, but not of the dragon. "I don't want any delights, sir dragon. I am questing for a black rose. Please give it to me and I will go."

"Then dismount and come in. Trust me, pretty little one, and receive your prize."

You have avoided looking at the amber eyes of

the beast, and Stardark snorts, dancing nervously between your legs. Dragons are notorious beasts. Should you trust this one or not?

1. If you decide not to, find Pathway 37 (page 147).
2. Turn to Pathway 20 (page 85) if your decision is to trust the beast.

PATHWAY 15

"I'll not be cornered like a witless coward," you mutter, and you set your feet firmly in the stirrups, hauling Stardark to a plunging halt. You've no idea how to use a staff or to unseat a man from a horse, but you hold it firmly as you drop the reins and kick Stardark right back into the paths of the desert warriors as they bear down on you.

They are a grim-faced, wild-looking crew, their blue-black hair held by leather thongs, their dark eyes narrowed as they charge at you. You whip the staff at the leader, missing him, but tearing his buckskin trousers and lashing into the rump of his mount. The horse lets out a squeal, veering away from you, and dumps his surprised rider.

As the man rolls in the dirt, the other riders circle and whoop, charging back at you.

This time, cruel smiles etch their faces, and the youth in front appears to be laughing!

You knee Stardark to a halt and wrap your hands

firmly about the staff, your knuckles showing whitely. But the youth brings his horse to a rearing stop, bright-colored silks in a rainbow hue about him, and he flings out his arm, hailing the others.

"Halt, riders of the Elash! This is no enemy."

The young man grins at you as his flaming red horse paws the ground and makes snorting challenges at Stardark. The older men rein in and crowd about him.

"Any stranger crossing without a pass is an enemy, Garon."

The youth shakes his head and says accusingly, "Go chase the ogres, Malthen, if you want to spill blood. This is a girl, though brave beyond her years, and your very eyes could tell you she is crossing the Elash out of desperation. Are you from Marcelayne?"

You can almost feel your eyes flash as you straighten in the saddle and point at all of the men. "Is this the way you treat your allies?"

The men laugh grudgingly as Garon says, "Without a doubt, she is from Marcelayne. Only King Joseph's daughters are so fiery of spirit."

The spears and bows are lowered, and horses curbed into quiet, as they toss their heads and eye the black stallion in their midst. Garon reaches out and wrests the staff from your hands. "Allies are risky business in these times, as Rastik has come out of the wastelands. His magic gives him the power to assume other shapes from time to time . . . and so we are wary about what we see and what we think we see."

You lift your chin as you toe Stardark into line with his chestnut, as the group urges their mounts from the canyon. "You don't need to tell me about Rastik," you answer clearly. "His army holds my family hostage."

"And you alone escaped? That explains the riders we spotted earlier."

You hate to cross the admiration ringing in Garon's voice, but you must tell the truth. "No, I didn't escape. But Rastik is a gambler, and my father wagered the safe surrender of the kingdom against him in a horserace."

"You?" The nomad youth looks at you, the sun glinting from the depths of his snapping black eyes, and then he breaks into howling laughter. Your lips tighten as you wonder if you were wise to trust him after all.

You refuse to say another word, even though Garon coaxes you for more of an explanation. You say only that you are tired and thirsty and will explain all when you've reached his camp. His stallion nips at yours as you trot across the rock and sands, toward a jumble of wagons and tents that grow out of the pink-and-gold horizon as though magically strewn there.

A herd of children greet you, pulling at the leggings of their relatives and whistling in greeting, their sharp sounds of joy gathering the women and other men, bringing them out of the horse herds and wagons, and the shelter of a few lone trees, to see what Garon has brought with him.

Sunburned and dirty, you self-consciously brush your heavy blond hair off your shoulders, wishing that you had brought comb or brush, then remembering that these people are not greeting you for your prettiness, but for your courage, as Garon tells them in short sentences of how he found you in the desert.

Long moments later, you are seated with a cup of water, resting on a silk cushion, as the camp gathers to hear your story. You tell it solemnly, stretching out the drink of water to last the entire length, knowing that you're not likely to get more soon.

As the last of your words fall into their thoughtful silence, you put the cup down.

Garon speaks first. "If this race is won, Rastik will retire from your country?"

"I . . . think so. There's a chance."

A tall, lean man, with a face weathered like fine leather, and a look of Garon about him, speaks. "It will take us many weeks to gather the nomads into an army fit to meet the ogrelord. This race is a better chance. Will you accept our aid, Princess Sarah, in winning it?"

It strikes you then that they know something you don't, and that with their help, you can effortlessly meet your pledge.

You are quiet, thinking furiously. But wouldn't that amount to cheating, and be just as underhanded, in a way, as Rastik is? Stardark is well rested now, and you think you are on the border of the Elash, so that you must be fairly close to the Garden of Galatea. He can win this race all by himself, and you feel pride for him burning in your every thought.

1. Will you take the aid of the desert nomads? Turn to your fate in Pathway 25 (page 103).

2. Or will you go on yourself, sure that you can win the race now? If this is your decision, find Pathway 48 (page 186).

PATHWAY 16

"Oh, bother," you say, and you climb over the garden wall to do it yourself, remembering that elves are indeed fickle creatures.

So upset are you with Tyrone that you never notice when the dragon's eyelid begins to flicker and the eye opens up, its amber gaze considering you wisely.

You freeze as you reach to pick a rose, and a deep, rolling voice behind you says, "Consider this well, maiden. Only one in love may touch that rose without dying."

Your heart does a funny bounce, but then you know that you qualify, for only that emotion encompasses all that you feel for Tyrone.

"But I am in love," you protest to the unseen dragon.

"Are you sure? Turn around and look at me, so that I may judge."

Without thinking, you turn and stare at the wily beast—and are caught by the magic of his gaze, even as Tyrone cries out, "No, Sarah, don't!"

Too late! You can feel yourself changing, changing into a willowy tree, even as Tyrone shouts and vaults the wall.

The elf stops before you as the dragon chuckles and falls back asleep, unconcerned by elves.

He touches your bark gently. "I'll be back, Sarah, to save you . . . but first, I'll take the rose to your family."

Impassively, you watch as he plucks the black-petaled object and leaves the garden, a fickle elf and a constant tree, and wonder if he will be back to see you again . . . sometime before the leaves turn.

IS THIS THE END?

PATHWAY
17

Nothing has been what it seemed since you got up this morning. Fearing the boy, you pull Stardark close and hug the tree. If you watch him long enough, you should be able to tell if he's just fishing or, well, just pretending he's fishing. Unless, of course, the fish aren't biting, and then . . . well, you'll just have to decide then if he's a spy or a poor fisherman.

Your head feels fuzzy with all these thoughts. "I'll just sit down here," you tell Stardark. "For a minute."

Before that minute is gone, your head is back against the trunk of the tree, and your mind is fading into a dark, dark sleep. You are vaguely aware that the stallion has gone to his knees and is lying on the ground next to you, and even the vast willow tree must be sleepy, for its bark-encrusted mouth is yawning, yawning . . .

You scream, as the mouth of the willow tree begins to close upon you!

Stardark rolls his eyes and weakly tries to get to

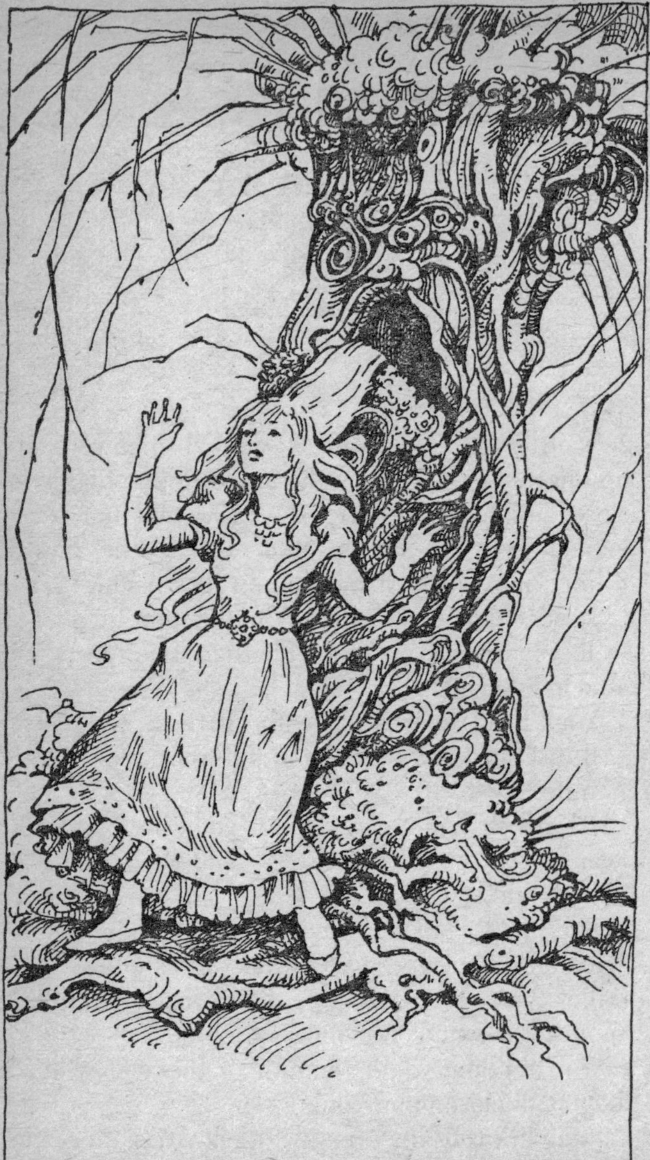

his feet, but cannot; he is as spindly on his legs as a newborn foal.

Willowman claps shut on your hair, and you are caught, your scalp pulled tightly as you scream again.

"Hey! Let her go!" The red-headed fisherman leaps into the glade, his bare fists flying as he pounds on the trunk of the tree. "Let her go, Old Man Willow, before I sing you into a forever sleep!"

There is a thrum and a hum, and then the bark lets go, and you pull your hair free, as both you and Stardark scramble to your feet and back away, fear surging through your hearts.

But the youth laughs as he puts his hands on his hips. "He'd have spit you out anyway. Old Man Willow's got no teeth and only eats a rabbit now and then. You're a mite big for him."

Staring suspiciously at the now quiet and non-threatening huge willow tree, you bite your lip. Hiding or not, now the youth knows you're here.

As if reading your thoughts, he looks at you. "Why don't you come with me? Your dress is soaked, and you're pale. I've got a jug of herb tea that should still be warm, and a patch of sun, which is hard to find in this old hole. Come with me."

You follow him reluctantly, shivering, and Stardark clomps along after you.

The boy throws you a grin over his shoulder. "I'm Neal, and unless I miss my guess, you must be one of King Joseph's daughters." He picks up his abandoned fishing pole, attempting to unravel the line.

73

A subject! He's from Marcelayne, too. But then, he wouldn't know. . . . You grab the spot of sunlight and hug your knees to you as you sit down, drying in the light.

"Yes. I'm Sarah, and thank you."

"That's all right. What are you doing way out here? Horse run away on you?"

"No," you answer sadly. "Neal, it's awful. The ogrelord Rastik invaded early this morning, and all my family is being held hostage."

He drops the fishing pole a second time. "Invaded! And you got free?"

"Something like that. Actually, well, it's rather complicated, but I'm in a race to get something, and if I get it and return in three days, Rastik has agreed to let my family go. If not, then my father will order all of his subjects to lay down their arms and submit to the invaders."

Neal whistles as he sits down on the river bank beside you. "Let me help, Sarah. I'm not much on kings and castles and such—all my family make their living from the swamp, from fish and hides and the like—but I'll help however I can. You're my princess!"

You smile at his earnestness, and think that he will grow to be a handsome man, in spite of the liberal dusting of freckles across his nose. "I don't know how you can help, unless you know the swamps well enough to guide me across, for I have to find the Garden of Galatea and bring back a black rose, before three days have passed."

Neal throws back his head and laughs. "And then what?"

"Why, Rastik has vowed to let us go, as I told you."

"No wonder the ogre soldiers have been tromping through here like hounds in search of a trail, and scaring all my fish. They're looking for you."

You fall silent, wondering if you have trusted this lad too much. The whole affair seems more amusing to him than serious. He laughs again and lays a warm hand across your chilled one.

"Trust me, Sarah . . . for the black rose grows in more than one place. I know of a bush right here in the swamps. You should be back home in your father's arms by nightfall." He jumps to his feet. "Follow me."

But you hesitate. His touch has disturbed you more that he can know—for his hands are not the rough, work-calloused hands of a freeman or a serf. No . . . he has done little hard labor more than you have, except perhaps to carry a sword or some such. No, Neal is not what he makes himself out to be, and you're very troubled.

A black rose grows, he says, somewhere in the swamps. But are you now to trust him or not?

1. If you go with Neal, turn to Pathway 1 (page 17).

2. Search out Pathway 31 (page 124) if you decide not to trust the fisherboy.

PATHWAY
18

You look at Garon's eager face. "I can take you through the passage," you say, "but not until dark."

"Then we wait! It is only a few hours."

Eruman frowns as he says, "I hope you know what you are doing, Garon."

The boy nods. "A water bag of the earth witch's potion, and Rastik will never know what hit him. With him down, his ogres will be too busy fighting each other to fight us!"

The nomad scratches his weather-burned jaw, then nods. "Yes, it might work at that."

By dark, you are huddled in the brush near the wall on the far side of the castle, Garon holding your elbow. The night air is chill, and you shiver, but the plains boy scarcely seems to notice it.

Then he says quietly, "I will not light the torch until we're inside."

You nod, remember he cannot see you too clearly, and husk out, "Okay."

Only the two of you are going in, for more

might make enough noise to alert Rastik. You rub your arms lightly.

As the last gray ray of twilight fades into darkness, you scamper from the brush to the wall and run your fingers over the stones, looking for the engraving that hides the lever which opens a small mouth.

The stone scrapes your fingertips until they are raw, as Garon dances impatiently beside you.

"What's wrong?"

"I can't find it!" you answer in panic.

"Take a deep breath. You told me your parents had taken you this way several times in practice. Now close your eyes and remember."

You do as bid, shaking inside, then the memory of the last time through the passage floods you. Shana stubbed her toe on a broken rock and cried for hours, it seemed.

You drop to the ground, feeling around. Garon drops beside you. "Look for a large, sharp rock half-buried in the ground!" That is, unless your father had it dug up!

"Ow! I think I found it," Garon says ruefully. He has moved almost a body length away from you. You join him and run your fingers over the stone.

"Yes! This is it!" Though your voices are pitched in whispers, you stifle your joy. Quickly you trace the crude carving, looking for the lever it conceals.

Thrummm—the rock vibrates as you pull the lever. There is silence for a moment after, as you and Garon press your ears to the rock. Then you can hear a balance moving, and a portion of the wall slides open.

It's like a dark maw into the castle depths, and you shudder. Garon pushes in after you quickly as you hurry inside. The passage is narrow; and even you must crouch over a bit—and all the better. If there are ogre soldiers inside guarding, they will be hampered by their size.

Click, click. Garon busies himself with the torch, and smoky, orange light flares out. You shudder as it reveals green-slimed walls, and cobwebs curl away with a *sssst* as they catch fire.

"Onward," he urges. The water bag of poison hangs across his back.

You hesitate, then lean forward. "A kiss for luck," you murmur and quickly brush his warm lips with your quivering ones. Then you turn and hurry down the passageway.

No one awaits to block you, though more than once Garon squashes a huge spider to bits, and once his quick dagger bites a large rat before it can bite you. As the passage spirals up into the castle, the walls grow warmer and cleaner.

You stop at the grating. The passageway is high now, and you straighten up in gratitude. "Haul the grating up, and a counterweight opens a panel in my mother's rooms."

"How likely is it that anyone will be there?"

You shrug. "I don't know."

Garon sets his jaw. "Then I'll be ready for anything!" Sinews on his bare arms ripple as he hauls the grating out of place, and a well-oiled panel clicks open.

You peer through it.

Your mother and Shana lie curled up on the bed, shivering with cold, for the room's fireplace is not lit. They are still shackled, and their eyes are closed in fitful sleep.

Shana's fly open as you step near.

"Sarah!"

"Shush!" You clasp your hand over her mouth quickly as your feisty little sister sits up.

You take your hand away. "Where is Rastik?"

She grimaces. "Probably in the hall, gambling with everybody else. I'm supposed to be serving him wine, but I won't! I won't! I won't do a thing for that nasty ogre. So he threw me in here with Mom. Says I can come out when I'm good, and he'll even have a fire lit for us then."

You smile. "Then I want you to call the guard and tell them you'll do it!"

"And you and he will bash him, right?"

Garon smiles. "Wrong, little one. But we have something to add to your wine!"

You and Garon hide under the immense bed of the queen as Shana does your bidding. You can hear the easy breathing of your mother, who only pretends to sleep now.

It is not pretending that Shana's teeth are chattering as she opens the huge door and calls out. "G-G-G-uards! I promise to be good. I'll take the wine down now."

A heavy foot and a snarl answer her. "Just in time, too! I'm on a roll, and the lord wants his wine now! Here!"

Cups rattle as a heavy platter is evidently thrust

into Shana's hands. She stammers as she adds, "May I get a cloak first? It—it's just as cold out there as it is in here!"

The ogre soldier laughs roughly. "We like it cold. Get it, but hurry!"

Shana sets the tray on the bed's coverlets, near your ready hands, as she goes to the armoire to get a shawl.

Quicker than the eye, Garon laces the wine jug with the earth witch's dangerous potion. He winks at Shana as she picks up the tray and makes her way down the hall.

Only moments later, you hear a great shout. "Rastik is dying!"

Ogre voices and tusks gnashing fill the air, as you and Garon creep to the door, his sword ready. Shana bolts into the room, her dark hair flying wildly about her small face.

"They're fighting to see who will take over!"

"Good!" Garon leaps into the hall. "In moments the gates will be open."

As his slim body disappears into the shadowy castle, you free your mother from her shackles, though picking the lock is not as easy as Garon had shown you earlier. She rubs her chafed wrists and then hugs both of you.

"You've done it, Sarah! You've freed all of us."

"Not quite." The three of you run to the balcony and there watch the boy, almost-man, hugging the shadows and racing to the front gate. All about him ogres are fighting hand to hand, and their terrible curses ring in the air.

Suddenly, the gates open, and a flood of horsemen

presses through, swords gleaming in the moon and torchlight.

"Ho! The Elash! The Elash have come!" their voices sing out in a mighty battle cry, and the ogres stop fighting with one another and turn and run.

There is a clank behind you, and the tall figure of your father joins you at the balcony, still chained, but standing tall and proud for all of that. He puts his arm about you and kisses your brow.

"You've done it, Sarah. You brought back an army."

Your mother adds softly, "More than that, dear. I think she brought back her own prince, too."

You blush, and the two of them laugh happily, as Marcelayne's streets are wiped clean of the ogre threat.

THE END

PATHWAY
19

You smooth down Stardark's mane. "You won't like this, boy, but we're going back! We need those water bags." With a bend of the reins, you turn the stallion around and head back slowly across the wastelands you just covered moments before, riding black lightning.

He does not protest until you near the area. Then he begins to snort, and his steps mince along the ground, his ears flatten to his head, telling you in his equine way that there is danger here and he doesn't approve of what you are doing. You must hammer your heels against his sides to keep him going, the reins held firmly in your hands to urge him on.

The pack and bags are scattered far and near across the sands. The desert lions evidently mauled their spoil with sharp and angry claws. One water bag is deflated, a dark puddle under it. You sigh as you dismount, then realize that one water bag is better than none at all.

You pull the stopper and squirt the precious

liquid into Stardark's muzzle as the stallion thirstily guzzles his ration. You allow yourself one squirt before you cap the skin again. Toeing the second skin, you see that it has been ripped open and is torn, useless to you now, even if you should find a well to refill it.

Your supplies are gone—nothing left but scraps and shreds of the saddlebag. An ironic smile colors the tone of your words as you say to Stardark, "I hope they liked stale jerky and hard biscuits!"

Better than nothing, but not the warm horseflesh and nibble of girl they anticipated! You lead Stardark to a boulder and remount, feeling a tinge of success. By coming back here, you did more than recover a water bag—you conquered your fear of the Elash, and replaced it with wariness.

As Stardark scrambles up a ridge, eager to put the scene of the ambush behind him, a whoop cuts through the air, startling both of you. You look over your shoulder as the horse cuts into the ground, lengthening his body out for another run.

Figures, men in skins and silks, their spears brandished, chasing you! A hunting party of nomads!

You lean over Stardark's neck, holding on for dear life, as the tired horse finds new speed in his long legs. But nomads are supposed to be friendly in the Elash, you think, as their hoarse cries pursue you. An arrow zinging past your head convinces you that allies are not always as reported.

Stardark turns into a dark, shadowy canyon, and you realize that you may be trapped. Whooping in triumph, the desert warriors stampede after you.

A shrub whips at your face, and as you claw it

aside, the long branch breaks off into your hand. For a second you think of tossing it down, but now you have a staff, and you may need a weapon of sorts.

Stardark whistles angrily, his nostrils cupped wide to suck in the hot, dry air. His steps don't falter, and you think that he may see an opening among the red desert rocks.

From what you know of the Elash nomads, they prize honor and courage among all other feats. If you turn Stardark and face them, they may recognize you are from Marcelayne and honor their tradition of being allies—or they may value your courage. Or they may simply stick you full of arrows and haul you back to their desert camp to do whatever it is they do with captives. You shudder as you think of ending up as a slave or maybe even someone's dinner!

Or you can give Stardark his head, and hope the wily stallion has spotted an escape route.

1. *If you fight, turn to Pathway 15 (page 64).*
2. *But if you wish to flee, then go on to Pathway 28 (page 116).*

PATHWAY 20

With a sigh, you answer, "I trust you, sir dragon, though for the life of me, I don't know why."

You enter through a swinging gate, though the wall is broken down enough that you could easily have vaulted it; it is no higher than Shana's back, which you jump playing leapfrog.

You reach the rose tree and pluck the flower, waiting all the time for the dragon to enchant you or devour you. But the beast does nothing, only watches as you take the flower. You turn and say, "Thank you, sir dragon, for this bud will save my family."

The dragon snorts proudly, eyes glinting, as it answers, "The gratitude is your test, for with that, you have free passage to leave. You'd be surprised how many enter, take what they want, and go without another word." The dragon blinks. "What's this? Tears?"

You can control yourself no longer. "With this rose, I must go home to free my family—and yet,

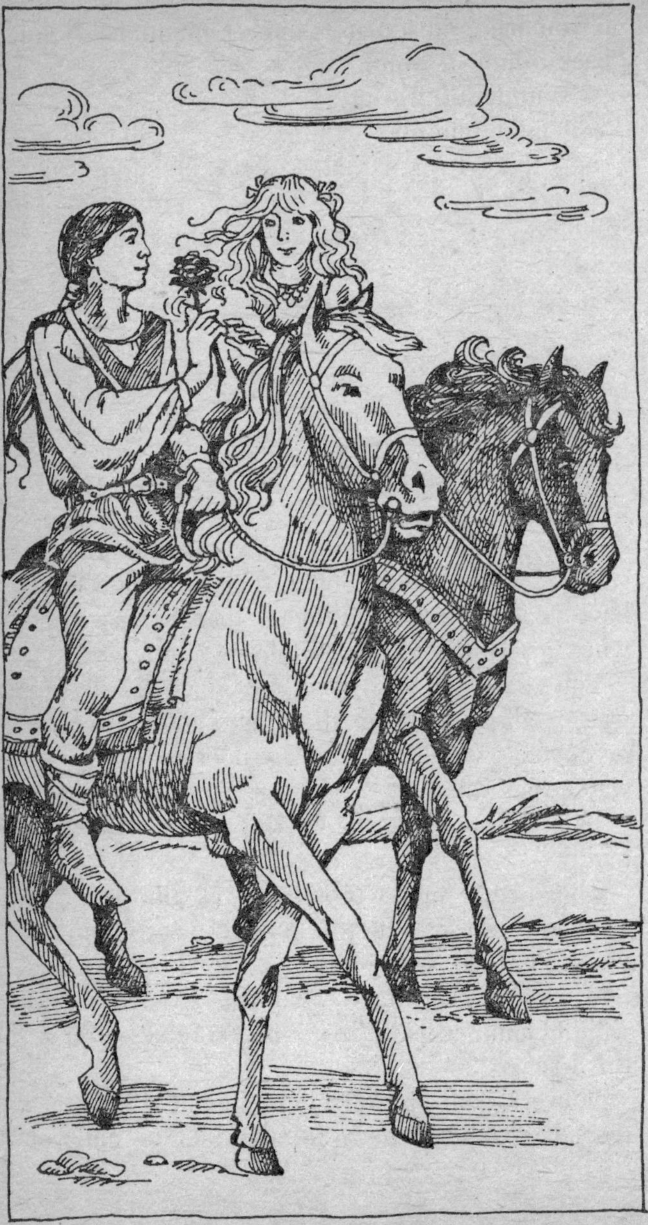

if you had refused it to me, I might have gone back to help Tyrone."

"Who is this Tyrone?"

"A mountain elf, a prince, who has helped me. And I think I . . . I think I might love him."

The dragon looks thoughtful. "Then I will help you, miss, but you must choose . . . home or elf."

1. If you ask the dragon to help you find Tyrone, turn to Pathway 42 (page 161).

2. But if you stay resolved to go home first, find Pathway 35 (page 138).

PATHWAY 21

You smooth the stallion's tangled mane under the reins. "Your speed will take us out of danger," you say. "The swamps it is! We've no time to waste!" And so you turn Stardark down the country lane which leads to the massive trees and dank bogs of the Manofee Hole . . . the Swamps of Despairing.

Stardark's smooth gliding walk buries the leagues behind you as you guide him past the dairy farms and groves. The swamps approach gradually, first as a tall, moss-covered tree here and there, and the long rush grasses. Then you notice that the hard-packed lane grows narrow and twisted, for no wagons use this road from out of the swamps. The ground becomes soft and mushy, and Stardark's hooves make a sucking noise as he strides along.

You shudder. Your bare-shouldered frock is hardly suitable for riding, and your toes are cramped in your slippers. If you only had your boots! Nasty buzzers dive at you, and you wave them away, as you and your horse walk farther into the darkening groves of the swamp.

Now many trees shoulder each other, rising out of the sluggish waters of the swamp. Pollen drifts along the water in thick yellow clumps, and a terrible smell wafts upward. You can't let Stardark drink here, no matter how safe it looks, for you know that some of the water has gone bad, and in some places poisonous snakes and reptiles lie hiding to attack unwary deer and wild pigs and other creatures that come to drink. Many are the stories your father has told you of the swamps, for he used to hunt here often when he was just a princeling. That was before the bogs swallowed up a hunting party, horses and all.

You rein the black horse to a stop and dismount carefully. Your slippers catch in the boggy ground. "Ugh." Carefully, you take down your water bag and, cupping your hand, painstakingly give your horse water. It's a slow process, and soon the front of your dress is nearly as wet as Stardark's muzzle. He gives an amused snort, sprinkling you more.

"Cut that out!" you say affectionately, and slap him on the neck. The water bag is tied back in place.

The horse pushes at you, nosing for a sugar lump. You tickle his muzzle. "Don't have any," you apologize. "But you'll get a chaliceful when we get home!"

Suddenly, the horse swings his head up, and his

ears prick forward. He has heard something in the swamps. You freeze too, listening with your lesser human senses. What could it be?

You pull Stardark into the slimy shade of a moss-covered branch, and the gray-green fauna hides you partially. Stardark's ears flick again, and then you spot what the animal has heard.

Horses. Their riders on foot, leading them over the soft ground carefully. Ogres, and tracking the path you've made into the swamp. You grind the leather reins into your palm.

So! Rastik doesn't intend for you to win fairly! He's sent soldiers after you in stealth. Quickly, you cup your hand over Stardark's nose before he can trumpet a greeting to the other horses. The stallion paws impatiently as you watch the ogres circle the ground.

You eye the sluggish waters behind the moss-covered tree. Let them try tracking you through that! You sniff. No evil smell here—the water's not poisonous, at least.

Quickly, you lead Stardark into the water. You shiver as its cold waves soak into your slippers and drag your skirts down, and the horse hesitantly steps in after you. Soon your followers are far behind as you follow the arm of the water deeper into the swamp.

Stardark nudges you onto the slippery banks and clambers out beside you. You shiver in the shadows and wring your petticoats as dry as you can. That ought to throw your trackers off! You've been in the water for over an hour. Unfortunately, you've thrown yourself off, too. The twisting river has taken you far from sight of the overgrown path you had been following. You're hopelessly lost.

You stand up and pat down your frock. Not hopeless! Princess or not, you've been listening to the stories around the castle. You know you can track your direction by the sun's course. Now if you can only find a clearing where the sun shines through!

You take Stardark's reins once more and guide him through the swamps.

The trees here are dark and twisted, with huge, gaping holes in their bark which look like dark mouths and eyes screaming at you. You can't control a shudder as their dead branches trail about you, sometimes pulling at your hair. More than once you snatch a ribbon back and retie it about your tangled locks. Stardark rolls his eyes nervously as he minces along behind you.

A low whistle stops you in your tracks. Sound where there should be none! A huge gray willow blocks your path, its trunk thick and squat, the spread of its drooping branches as large as a small cottage. Somewhere on the other side is the whistler. More of Rastik's ogre soldiers? You shudder. Just when you thought you'd outsmarted them!

You stroke your horse's black muzzle. "Quiet, Star. I have to find out who that is," you whisper.

The horse follows you to the trunk of the willow. You can hear noises on the other side. A river flows swiftly past, its blue water cheerful-looking after the slower, dank waters of the swamps. Something splashes, and you hear a series of noises that make you frown. What can possibly be doing something on the other side of the tree?

You lean around, very carefully, to look.

It's a boy! Well, not really a boy, for he's taller than you, and his peasant pants are much too short for him. He stands on the riverbank, the sun glinting off his reddish hair. His shirtsleeves are rolled to the elbow, and his vest is decorated with pins of different kinds. You squint—no, hooks! Fishing hooks! The boy is fishing. You see the pole in his hand now, and the nearly invisible string heading into the river. A basket pack rests on the ground beside his bare feet, and his boots are drying in a little ray of sunshine that glimmers through the swamp.

The sun! Now you have caught your sign. But still, you're deep in the swamps. The fisherboy looks quite at home here. He could probably help you if you asked.

On the other hand, he could be a decoy for Rastik! "Oh," you groan. "I'm no good at this!"

If you watch him long enough, you could probably tell if he is for real, or if he is another spy looking for you. Or you can quit wasting time and hail him now, asking for help . . . before the sun glints too low in the sky. The first day is passing! You must hurry!

92

Stardark nudges your leg as though to urge you to decide. You hug the willow tree closer. What to do?

1. If you decide to hide and make sure the fisherboy is friendly, turn to Pathway 17 (page 71).

2. If you hail him now, go to Pathway 26 (page 108).

PATHWAY 22

Tears welling in your eyes, you shake your head. "Tyrone . . . I will never forget the magic of these past days, or that I do love you . . . but you are an elf, and your days are years, and I can't chain you to a mortal. I will go on without you, but I'll never forget you."

And with a shout, you turn your back on the prince and kick Stardark, plunging him into a gallop down to the city gates, never to look back, except in memories.

THE END

PATHWAY 23

You put your hand on Garon's wrist as he reins back Arrow. "Let me down. And when I've loosened him, let him go . . . and me."

"You?"

With a sigh, you nod. "I must do this as I pledged, Garon. If there is a dragon, I will meet it alone. You do understand, don't you?"

"Your honor." He says it stiffly.

"Not to mention what a dragon might do if you came riding up like a nomad warrior, ready to send a lance through its heart. No . . . I think it's better if I go on alone. You wait here. If I come back, I'll need your help again."

At that he smiles, and lets you gracefully down to the ground.

Stardark doesn't come when you whistle, but remains frozen in his tracks, a graceful statue. His skin shivers slightly as you walk up to him and rub your hand lightly over his hot and sweaty hide.

"You can't carry me any farther, Star . . . and now your heart is elsewhere," you murmur to him. Then, quickly, before you can change your mind, you ungirth the saddle and let it fall to the ground.

His head is still high, as you pull the bridle off, and he stands for just a second, freed of all manmade restraints.

"Go!" You slap his neck and startle him into bolting away. Then the black stallion trumpets a challenging neigh and follows after the herd of wild horses, the untamed, as Garon called them. The limp in his stride is barely noticeable, and you can only pray that he will be fully healed one day.

Garon says nothing as you walk past him. He has dismounted, and is resting cross-legged in the grasses, Arrow hobbled beside him. As you mount the crest, you can see the green expanse of the Garden waiting a league away.

Your feet are sore in your thin slippers by the time you arrive near the Garden's edge. There is a low stone wall, but you can see trees blossoming and you can hear the sound of running water. There is no sign of any dragon.

What a difference a league has made! Green, green all around, like your beloved Marcelayne. Why would the nomads live in the desert and plains when this lush paradise is so close?

But as you look around, it's obvious it wouldn't hold the proud tribe of Garon's people. It's much too small. This is only one small valley in a jumble of sharp rocks, at the foot of the Dynas Mountains. Beyond is the tip edge of the elves' domain, and to one end, part of the swamp of the Manofee Hole snakes down. No, the Garden is only a tiny parcel of land.

But a big enough parcel, you discover as you tiptoe to the wall and look over, to hold a sleeping dragon.

Bother! And worse words tumble through your brain. You can see clearly the blooming trees ahead of you, in the center of the lovely garden, and one of them blooms with roses so deep a blue that they might be black . . . like the hair of Garon's people. Curled about the base of the tree is a green dragon, sleek and young, with its wings folded neatly about it, its crown of spines rattling as it snores lightly. The wood nymph is nowhere in sight, not that she'd be likely to help you anyway. Nymphs are a flighty folk.

And though the dragon is young, its bulk is considerable.

You sigh. Maybe if you circle the garden wall, you might be able to get closer to the tree . . . but as you turn, your torn and dusty petticoats brush the stones, and the very rocks cry out.

"Thief! Thief!"

You stomp your foot. "Shut up!" you say as the rock wall bellows loud enough to wake the dead . . . or a sleeping dragon.

"Whuff!" The beast draws to its full length and rises to its scaled height, turning amber eyes in your direction. The stones immediately become quiet as proper stones ought to, their job of alerting the dragon finished.

You don't stare the dragon in the eyes, wary of all you have heard of dragon magic.

"What do I sniff?" says the dragon, in a low voice, like the wind over the reeds, hollow and suggestive of deep under the earth in secret places. The creature approaches you, the sun glinting off its bright-green scales and smoking eyes. "A maiden!" it answers itself in delight. "Pink and tender, waiting for me." Its jaws open, and its forked tongue slithers out in anticipation.

No sword! No armor! How to fight this beast? But you freeze by the rock wall, thinking of nothing you can do, for all you know how to do is princessly things like embroidering, and arranging the menu, and—and singing!

Singing! That's it! Music to soothe the savage beast. You take a deep breath, close your eyes, and begin to sing.

The ground shakes as the huge beast draws closer, but you ignore it. You'd rather not see if its nostrils flare red, if its mouth opens to flame you, as you sing of spring, and flowers, and falling in love. Your voice shakes at first, and you're terribly thirsty, but your song gains in strength as you think of Garon, and Stardark, and your family.

All other noise stops while you sing with all your heart.

There is silence when you've finished, and you find the courage to open your eyes.

The dragon is draped over the stone wall, eyes half closed, purring in pleasure. It finishes its climb and falls at your feet.

"Order and I will obey," the large worm sighs. "Your voice has enchanted me."

You let out a shout of joy. You've won! The

black rose will scarcely wilt at all, for you will return home on dragonwing, and let Rastik beware your wrath if he tries to cross you!

Being a princess is good for some things, you think, as you climb over the wall and pick the rose. The dragon probably would have roasted a prince, armor and all.

THE END

PATHWAY 24

"What choice have I?" you say, and tears well in your eyes at the terrifying thought. "I will go with you in the morning."

"Good." Tyrone takes you up in his arms and carries you across the field, as though he knows that you are suddenly too weary to walk. "In the morrow, then!"

You scarcely know when he enters a spiral building and lays you gently on a down bed, softer than any other in the world that you have ever slept in.

Bells wake you in the morning. Your pink dress has been mended and cleaned, and your petticoats, too, and they lie at the foot of the bed, with an exquisite rose pink cloak over them, of elfin weave. You dress quickly, and Tyrone is outside waiting for you, dressed somewhat more somberly than the day before, but no less finely.

Stardark is also waiting and whickers in greeting as you step to his head and scratch his jaw in his favorite place.

Though you should be tired and bone-weary

from the night of merrymaking, you have never felt better. Tyrone smiles as he pulls the cloak over your shoulders.

"It will keep out the mountain chills, and more. It will turn aside most blades, and hide you if you should need to be hidden. It will remind you day in and day out that you are l—" He stops suddenly, and his face changes. "That is," he says. "It will remind you of the elves."

How strange. He was going to say "loved," you think with wonder, as he strides away, adding, "Follow me, and quickly. We have no time to waste."

You hurry after him, and the village is left behind. It looks, in the daylight, as you turn and watch it over your shoulder, only a little less magical than at night, for its silver and gold towers point at the sky, and the sun seems to warm here more than anywhere. With a shiver, you step after Tyrone, for he stands in the mouth of a mine shaft, leading into the mountainside.

The tunnel becomes dank and stale, and it leads downward, ever downward, curling and twisting. More than once you cry out and stumble and fall into Tyrone, who catches you and apologizes.

"I have the sight and can see in the dark. I'm sorry, Sarah, but if you carry a torch, you'll blind me."

"Then be my eyes for me," you say, and his hand catches you roughly and pulls you to him. There is a breath-stopping moment when his chest is pressed to yours, then the elf pulls away, holding only your hand, as he guides you down into the mines. You lose all sense of time.

Stardark follows behind, his pursuit of you ever slower, and as you stop to pet the horse, you find him shivering and lathered in fear. His nostrils flare as he scents something you cannot.

"Tyrone, he's afraid. I don't think he'll go any farther."

The elf prince has pulled his sword, and the blade gleams faintly, an alarm of some sort. Perhaps goblins are near.

You pull on Stardark's reins, but the horse throws his head high, plants his hooves, and refuses to go on.

"Then leave him," the elf says tightly. "Our voices echo in here like drums. We have come more than halfway, and can't turn back now. He'll be safe—I pledge it."

"No . . . I can't do that. When we reach the Garden, I'll still need to return home. And suppose he wanders back the wrong tunnel, and is stuck in here, or goblins pull him down?"

Tyrone's voice lowers dangerously. "A second time you do this to me. An elf's honor is his word. If I have said he'll be safe, he will. Only leave the stubborn beast where he is and follow me—and hurry!"

1. *If you leave Stardark, turn to Pathway 2 (page 20).*

2. *But if you try to bring him on, go to Pathway 14 (page 61).*

PATHWAY
25

With a flush, you answer in a low voice, "My pride says no, but many a country has fallen because of pride. I came to the Elash in hopes that I could find your people. Please . . . I would be happy to accept whatever help you can give."

Garon jumps to his feet and bows. "Then mount Stardark and head back to your country's borders. I, or one of the Elash riders, will join with you . . . carrying a black rose."

"But how—"

Even as you speak, a drum sounds, boom-booming its mysterious message across the plains.

"What are they saying?"

"We are calling our riders, and those from other encampments. We will form a living road across the wastes to the Garden of Galatea and bring your rose back to you. Each man will ride until his mount is spent, then pass the burden along, and so we may more speedily cross the Elash than a single rider trying to conserve his horse's endurance."

A tear trembles at the corner of your eye as you realize the awful race will be over soon. You stand up, with Garon's help. "Thank you," you say, realizing that it doesn't seem to be enough.

But Garon reaches out and touches the teardrop, and the moisture glistens on his rough fingertip. "Water! She gives us water in gratitude!"

The nomads shout in one mighty voice, and you understand that water is so precious here that crying is not a luxury allowed to them. Stardark is led up to you, his black hide cleaned and glistening, and you are tossed aboard by Garon's lean but strong arms.

He holds on to your waist a little longer than he might, and smiles, and you are struck by the handsomeness of the nomad prince.

"In the spring, perhaps I will travel to Marcelayne and see how our alliance can be strengthened."

A shy smile curves your lips, and you feel a blush travel across your face. "Perhaps," you murmur as you kick Stardark into a trot, leaving the encampment of the riders behind.

Hours later, the sun is slanted nearly below the horizon when a rider bearing a torch thunders up behind you, and you recognize his form before the chestnut rears to a halt and exchanges greetings with Stardark.

Garon holds the black rose out to you. Its velvety form is perfect, a bud just beginning to open, and it shows no sign of the desert heat.

You take it gently. "How can I . . ."

He holds up his hand, solemn and quiet. "You have already thanked us, by regarding us as friends

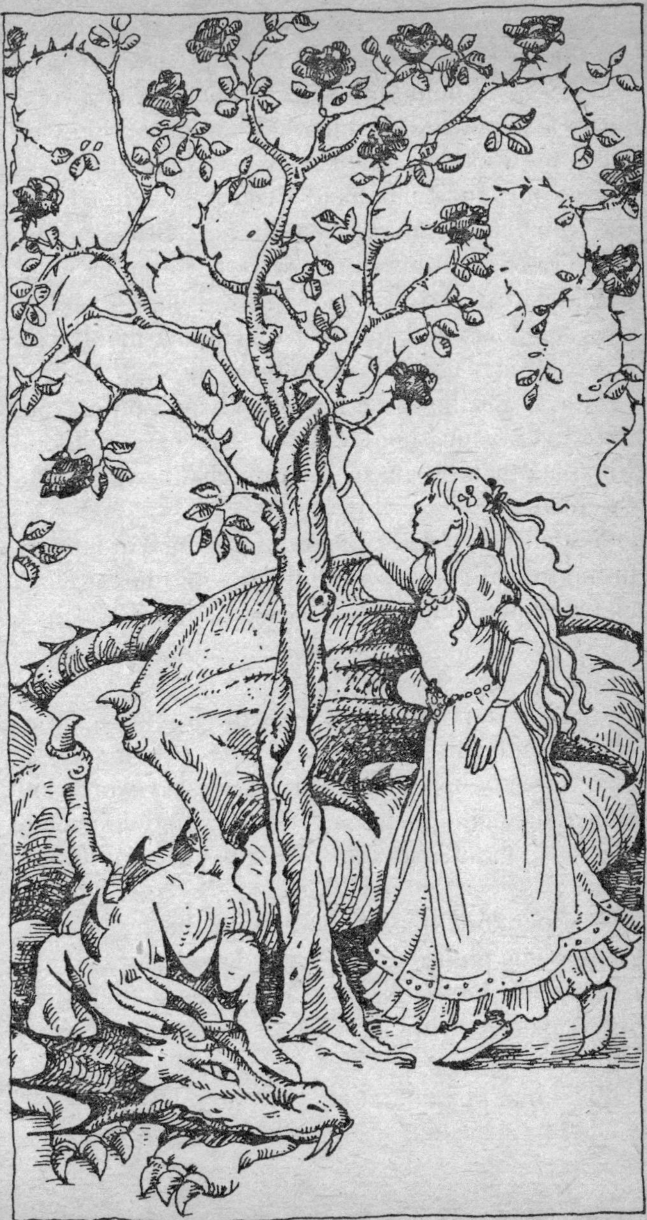

and allies, and giving us the honor of your tears. But for myself . . ." And at this the youth gives a smile, and its light flashes across his face, and your heart feels a little peculiar. "I hope that you can make me welcome when I come visiting."

Or courting? Your hand shakes as you pick up the reins once more. "I will try, Garon," you answer softly. You kick Stardark onto the familiar road, leaving the dry knolls of the border of the two kingdoms and hurtling downward to Marcelayne, beautiful and lush Marcelayne.

Shouts and hoarse cries follow you, and as you look over your shoulder, you see ogre soldiers whipping their exhausted mounts, chasing you down the road.

With a cry of glee, you urge Stardark to let out his speed, and you lead the ogres into town, clattering down the cobbled lane as windows and doors fly open.

"The princess! It's Sarah!"

Cries of happiness and triumph greet you, in a blur of lanternlight and color, as Stardark speeds you toward the palace. He needs no words of encouragement, as his hooves strike sparks upon the road, and the soldiers of Rastik pour out of the castle.

The ogrelord himself bounds to the top of the steps as you plunge to a halt and dismount, Stardark rearing, his hooves keeping the ogres at their distance. You hold the black rose in triumph above your head.

"The race is won!"

Shana speeds out of the palace door, her chains

rattling as she skids to a halt, crying, "She won! She won! She beat you, Rastik!"

The beast says nothing, but stands, gnashing his tusks, and a purple stain grows up his face, starting at the neck and edging upward through the warts and hairs and battle scars.

Then Rastik roars and pounds his fists in anger, and with a *poof!* he disappears, leaving only Shana there in surprise.

"Did I do that?" she asks quietly, as you laugh to see the ogre soldiers scrambling to leave the palace grounds, dropping weapons and running in confusion because their lord has destroyed himself in a fit of temper.

You hug her as you say, "I think, in a way, you did!"

THIS IS THE END OF THIS ADVENTURE.

PATHWAY 26

You shake yourself impatiently. "Don't be such a scaredy-cat," you scold yourself. And you step out behind the tree, calling, "Hello there."

The youth whips around, surprise opening his blue-green eyes wide and nearly scattering the freckles off his face.

"Who are you? And where did you come from?"

"Out of the swamps, and I'm lost." Stardark comes up behind you and whickers, impatient for a drink of that fresh river water.

The youth drops his pole and pulls aside his belongings, to relinquish the patch of sunlight to you. "Here . . . sit here and warm yourself." He opens his fishing basket to produce a stoppered clay jug, which he presses into your hands. You can feel the warmth as he says, "Herb tea. Please, drink all you want."

You drink thirstily, then pass the jug to him, with a smile, as the liquid fills you with warmth and well-being. "I don't think I've ever tasted anything better."

"I'm Neal . . . and I'm willing to bet you're the one the ogres are chasing. What's happened?"

"I'm Princess Sarah, and Rastik and his army of ogre soldiers invaded the kingdom this morning."

"And you escaped?"

"Not quite. Rastik's a gambler, and I've bet his hold on Marcelayne against my winning a race. It's hard to explain, but—"

He holds up a hand, and despite your tiredness, you think that he will someday be a handsome man. "Don't, then. How can I help, your highness?"

"Do you know the swamp well?"

Neal smiles. "I'd be a poor fisherman if I didn't. Still, the Manofee Hole is a treacherous place. Where do you need to go?"

"It's called the Garden of Galatea."

He nods briskly as he restoppers the jug and puts it away, along with his fishing equipment. Then he pulls his boots on. "This river runs into a freshlet there. In the other direction, it draws right up to the lake behind your palace, your highness."

"Really?" You look at the water thoughtfully. If you had but known that and had a boat . . .

Stardark shakes his head vigorously, and you pat the horse. You swat a biter as it lands on your arm, nipping you hard enough to leave a droplet of blood behind.

"Stick close with me, then, and I'll lead you on. Wait a minute while I get my boat."

"Boat?" you echo, wondering if he has read your thoughts.

But the boat he pulls out from under a sheltering branch is little more than a bark, a small shell of a boat for one person. You might be able to get in, but Stardark would most certainly be left behind. So much for your plans, you think, as he tugs on the rope.

The three of you walk down the river, Neal asking you of events at the palace, and you filling in all that you know. His eyes flash as you tell him of Rastik's plundering of the castle you call home.

"I would wring his neck if I caught him!" the youth exclaims.

You smile bitterly. "It would take stronger hands than yours. Still, if I'm successful, you will have helped!"

Suddenly, Neal freezes and grasps at your arm. He lets go long enough to tie up the boat, then leads you and Stardark into the swamp, away from the river. Before you can ask why, the ugly sound of ogre voices fills the air, in the harsh, clacking language that they speak to each other.

You find yourself shivering as they pass by unaware of you. Neal sees your fear and says, "We'll have to stay away from the river for a while."

And so you follow him into the depths of the swamp. The day grows dimmer and dimmer and the swamp thicker. Birds scream past with a flash of their wings, and leather-skinned creatures groan and slide away into pools of water as you step near.

Suddenly, Stardark loses his balance on the path behind you and slips into a stagnant pool of water. You tug on his reins, and the horse thrashes, unable to clamber out of the muddy pool.

Fear strikes your heart. Neal signals you to be quiet, as ogre voices once again grow loud, and you put your hand out to Stardark to quiet his thrashing.

Long moments go by, and then the ogres are gone again. You turn, your heart like stone, to see Stardark sunk to his withers in the quicksand pool.

Neal takes the reins from your hands. "We can't get him out," he says quietly. "And if we try, our efforts will bring the ogres back."

"I can't leave him! He—he'll be sucked under, and die!"

The youth looks at you in understanding, but answers you, "What is one horse compared to your family and your kingdom?"

You can't answer him, because in his way he's right.

Stardark looks at you, his large brown eyes ringed with the white of fear, as his nostrils flare, and he stretches his neck to keep above water.

1. If you leave Stardark, go to Pathway 29 (page 118).

2. Turn to Pathway 11 (page 51) if you try to rescue your faithful horse.

PATHWAY 27

You knee Stardark forward, to the wall's edge. It is broken in several places, and there your stallion can easily stride over it; in others it is chest-high, but even then you know Stardark could jump it easily. If a horse could make it in and out so comfortably, what purpose for the wall? It does not contain the dragon . . . or does it?

You avert your eyes, to avoid being mesmerized by the beast, as it sings out, in a hollow and strangely beautiful voice, "Who comes here?"

Perhaps there is a way to be reasonable with this animal. "I—I do. I've come for mint to cool my face and hands. I've ridden across the Elash desert and I'm sunburned. And I look for water for my horse." Your voice, trembling at first, goes stronger and sounds braver than you feel.

The dragon settles a little, examining its front claws. Then it shakes its head, rattling its spines, as it declares, "You are a liar as well as a thief. You've come for one of my magical flowers."

You gasp, and as you stammer for an answer,

Stardark suddenly lets out a high-pitched whistle of anger. His ears flatten as he sails over the wall, plunging to a halt right at the dragon's nostrils.

The creature hisses and curls back, striking like a snake, fangs glistening, but Stardark is too quick for it, as you hang onto the saddle horn and his mane for dear life.

They curl and pounce at one another, thrashing life and death below your feet, as you are little more than a burr in Stardark's mane, black and emerald striking and jabbing. Then the dragon sinks back, hissing madly, and you see its green flanks begin to swell as it inhales deeply.

You saw at the reins, trying to regain control of the maddened horse. "Star! It's going to breathe fire! Run, run!"

But the stallion takes no notice of you as he rears to lash out again, and your heart stops drumming in your chest, for you know you're about to be blasted to ash, the both of you.

The dragon's jaws open, the tongue red-hot and lolling between ivory fangs, and the creature begins to breathe.

Nothing issues but a foul-smelling smoke, and you cough madly as Stardark drops to his fours and snorts and chokes. The dragon pants and says, "Damned dragon form, anyhow!"

You know that voice! But before you can do anything, your horse rears again, his hooves windmilling through the air, and the dragon scrambles away, rearing itself to its height, wings unfurled.

The tree of black roses is at its back—a tall, slim-trunked tree with branches sculpted to a round

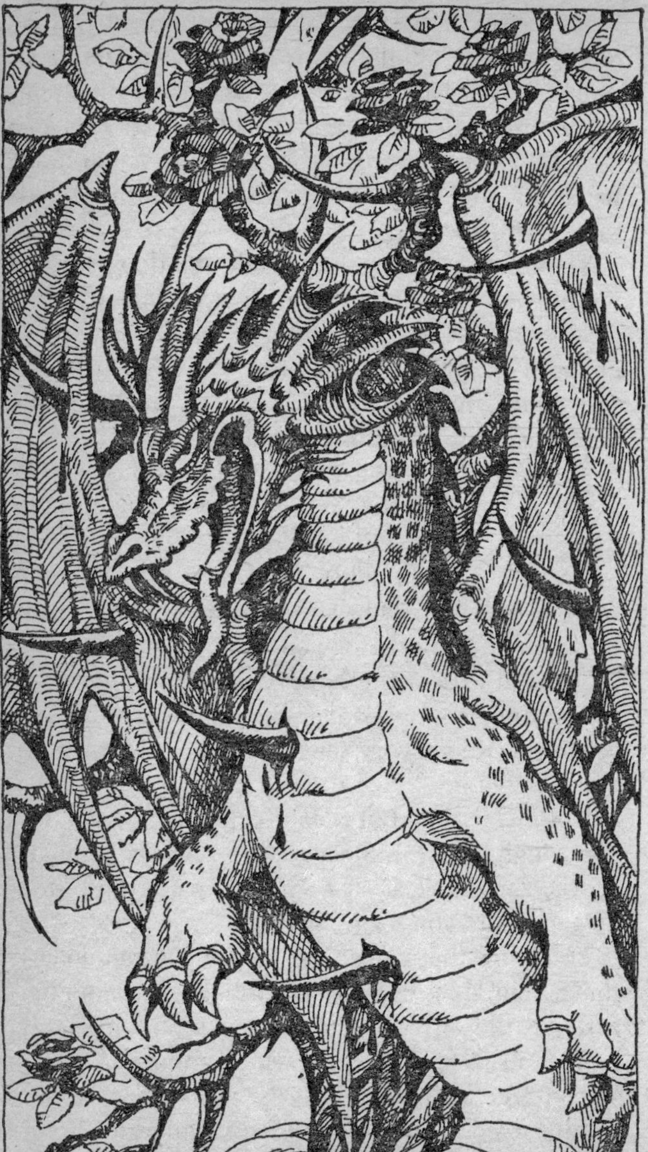

shape, and thorns in its bark as long as short swords. For a moment, everything is frozen, you desperately hanging on to Stardark, the proud stallion rearing, the dragon on its hind feet, toppling backward into the rose tree.

Then a death scream of agony breaks the enchantment, as Stardark plunges into the dragon, and it's impaled on the rose tree, and hangs there, writhing in distress, and then the beast is silent.

You gasp in amazement as the dragon form ripples away, and you see Rastik impaled there, caught in his own enchantment gone awry, caught by his own magic and his desire to win a bet, no matter what the cost.

You feel sorrow for only a moment, for the ogre overlord was evil, and would have destroyed all of your family and kingdom. Then you rein Stardark away and leave the Garden of Galatea, after first plucking a black rose for yourself.

Its fragrance makes the journey home seem much shorter and sweeter.

THE END

PATHWAY 28

You can't fight! In desperation, you whip Stardark faster, and head him into the shadowed depth of the canyon.

But the stallion has a mind of his own. He plunges to the walls and begins to climb, the soft red dirt crumbling under his hooves. You nearly slide off backward, and grab frantically for his mane, half off the saddle and half on, as the horse literally climbs the canyon wall. At the top, he whirls and takes off across the wasteland as you right yourself, thrusting your feet back into the stirrups.

The Elash warriors are left far behind, in pink-and-yellow dust, by Stardark's ever-lengthening strides. He carries you over the border and stands, sides heaving, once more in Marcelayne. You dismount and walk him to the road, to the side of the small brook, and let him drink his fill.

With determination, you mount up and return to the fork in the road, where you made your decision to go to the desert. Now only the swamps and mountains remain as an option, and the day is already noon!

You sigh, staring at the paths. The Swamps of Despairing are dreadful indeed, and you are afraid to go, but the Dynas Mountains are little choice to comfort you.

1. If you go to the swamps, see Pathway 39 (page 152).

2. Find Pathway 5 (page 29) if you take the road to the mountains.

PATHWAY
29

Heartbroken, you let Neal take the reins from you, and he drops them into the pool of water, as Stardark gives a long, quavering whicker.

You can't even reach him, for as you try, the bank crumbles under you, threatening to throw you into the quicksand pool, too. Neal grabs your elbow. "Let's go, and hurry!"

Blinded by tears, you stumble after Neal into the swamp, with no heart to see the last of your valiant horse taken by the quicksand.

You can go no farther when you stop by the river, gasping, tears overflowing your eyes silently, your face wet with your grief. Neal hesitates, then says, "Maybe I can boat you there."

You shake your head and cup your hands to hide your face, muttering, "I'll be all right in a minute. If only I had the black rose!"

He puts his arm about you to console you, and you are aware of the warmth and strength of his body close to yours as he says, "Please . . . please don't weep."

But you must, for you have no choice, and when you withdraw your face from your hands, the tears have pooled there, and glisten in the dim light of the swamp.

Neal cups his underneath as he says, in an awed voice, "Look!"

For the tears are growing solid, and darkening, and even as you gasp in surprise, a black rose lies there, as if by magic.

He takes his hand away and says, "You are indeed a princess. My boat! Now we can use the boat," he adds in triumph.

Carefully, the two of you get into the leaflike vessel, and he quickly puts it into the current of swiftly flowing water to the city. You've won, though your heart is as broken as if you'd lost, and you try to smile as you listen to Neal. He tells you he is not a fisherboy, but a prince come to see if the daughters of King Joseph are truly as beautiful as he has heard . . . but that's another story.

THE END

PATHWAY
30

You shudder, as you remember the stealthy silence with which the lions stalked you. "I don't want to go back," you tell your tired horse as you stroke his neck.

He lifts his head, as though agreeing, and you turn him to the left, to cross back over the wilderness to the trade road. You will risk running into the three riders sent after you, but now you have no choice, as the only wells you know of are along that road.

The hot wind and sun tear at you. Your skin feels like a drum tightening over the bones of your face. The tip of your nose must be sunburned by now, you think. You try to think of something else besides being hot and tired and thirsty.

"When we get back, I shall reward you," you tell Stardark. "With fresh grain and mountain clover—and apples! You will have three large, shiny apples—one for each day—all crisp and red and juicy." You stop. This isn't working! You can hardly talk for thinking of the juicy apples.

Then you ride in silence, refusing to think of other things but your current mathematics lesson, as Stardark's long dark legs eat up the distance.

For a while you dismount and walk beside the stallion, giving him a rest. It also gives you a chance to see the tiny creatures that inhabit this part of the wilderness, tawny little bodies with sharp black noses and sparkling eyes and little whisks of tails that dart in and out of their holes to look at you, sitting up on their hind legs, looking like plump merchants eyeing a potential buyer. With a whistle, they will all disappear at once into their holes, but only a few feet farther and they will pop up again, as though trying to decide if you are friend or foe. Stardark rolls his eyes at their antics at first, startled when the entire colony pops up for a look, but then he ignores them, his head bobbing as he walks at reins' length.

Your tongue feels like cotton in your mouth when at last you approach a broken hill, hoping that the trade road lies just beyond it. You secure the reins to a shrub as you climb the sand and rock, for Stardark's black form will stand out clearly, and you don't know if the ogre soldiers are beyond or not.

You crawl to the top and lie down to look over, sighing as your beautiful dress gets even dirtier. "Find a well," you say to yourself. "First I'll drink from it—and then I'll bathe in it, dress and all!"

As you look down, you see in amazement that you are practically on top of the trade road—and there is the encampment of the dark riders, their horses hobbled, and a tent pitched. They are waiting out the heat of the midday, perhaps—or just waiting for you to ride along so that they can pick up your trail again, for their camp would be hidden to riders along the road just beyond. You chew your lip. It might be possible to sneak up and steal one of those water bags piled behind the tent, as the ogres are playing at sticks and stones and arguing loudly, their voices reaching you on the ridge.

But that would be terribly risky. If you were small and quick, like Shana—who always excels at hide and seek—you might try it.

As you turn away, a flash catches the corner of your right eye. You look far behind, down the road and more so, to a shining reflection against the desert, catching the midday sun.

Water! It has to be a water spot, so flat and shiny. Your heart does a funny thump. It could be a mirage—a trick of the sand and sun—but you don't think so. You know there is a well or two along the road. It's far away, but you think Stardark can reach it. After all, horses can travel for a day or two without water, and he hasn't gone nearly that long yet. You could be there before late afternoon.

But then again . . . it is still along the road, and you know from the sight of Rastik's minions camped below you that you must leave the road and hope to find the nomads and ask for their help.

You pause. Either way, you must have water!

1. If you decide to steal the water bags, go to Pathway 34 (page 131).

2. Turn to Pathway 8 (page 44) if you decide to go on to find the oasis.

PATHWAY 31

You pull to your feet, grasping Stardark's reins. A moment of panic seizes you as Neal grabs for your hand.

"No! I won't go anywhere with you . . . I don't even know who you are," you cry, plunging away from him and jumping into Stardark's saddle.

As the youth reaches for you, crying, "Wait," you whip Star across the neck with the reins, and he lunges out, knocking the boy aside and racing deep into the forest.

In moments, you are lost deep in the darkening swamp, gasping for breath, your heart pounding. Stardark halts, shuddering, as mosquitoes snipe at both of you.

Two forms rise out of the mists, and Rastik's ogre soldiers laugh heartily. "Found yer at last, miss! Now, come along with us, and there'll be no trouble . . . no trouble at all," the first one growls.

The second adds, gnashing his tusks, as he takes Stardark's reins from your numb hands, "Rastik's never lost a bet yet!"

THIS IS THE END OF THIS ADVENTURE.

PATHWAY
32

You look at Tyrone. After all, he has just saved your life. You shudder as your eyes pass over the bloody goblin corpses not far away. You take his arm. "I'll go with you for the moment, but please—send someone after my horse as soon as possible."

"Without a doubt," the elf says, "for though he is not of our bloodline, he is a remarkable animal. Ah, you are cold and shiver. I have forgotten that mortals find the mountains chill. We will soon be at our demesne, and I'll get a cloak and warmer clothes for you."

"Don't you get cold?" you ask, as he helps you over the path and into the forest, among the pine trees, onto a path you never could have seen on your own.

Tyrone smiles brightly. "Not in the way that you do," he answers. His aid over the mountain path is more than just one of steadying you, for he seems to give wing to your steps, and you are running lightly beside him, forgetting the bruises and ordeals of having been half the day and more in the saddle. For a dizzying moment, you wonder what it would be like to be dancing with him, lighter than air.

The elf village appears suddenly before you, and shouts ring out, melodious voices, in elfin language, and forms surround you. Tyrone's grip grows tight on your arm as he answers, and you gasp as you look about—for the elves are clearly preparing for war, their armor and weapons stacked about, and horses picketed at one end of the woods.

Tyrone smiles nastily as he says, "Ah, yes, my dear. And you are but the first spoil of our conquest against Joseph the Younger. It has taken us centuries, but we will have our revenge."

Your heart sinks as you realize you have fled from one invader straight into the arms of another.

THE END OF YOUR ADVENTURE

PATHWAY
33

You smile at Neal. "Well . . . you did come this far. But after we reach the Garden of Galatea, I don't know what we can do."

He smiles mysteriously. "My boat was given me by the faeries. We shall see what we shall see."

At that, he takes your hand and climbs up on Stardark's rump, fishing pole, basket, and all. As he slides one arm about your waist to steady himself, you feel strange. You're aware that he is taller than you, and handsome, and despite his rough ways and talk, he's not like any freeman you've ever met before. There is something more to Neal than just being a fisherman.

Without another word, the two of you ride down into the valley. There Neal makes camp and shares the remains of his packed lunch, for it is night now, and you set Stardark out to graze. By the light of the fire, he keeps you merry with jokes about the fish he's almost caught, and when you go to sleep, it is with a lighter heart.

In the morning, he has Stardark groomed and

watered, and ready for you. The stallion nuzzles Neal's sleeve affectionately, and you feel a pang of jealousy, for the horse has never taken to anyone but you. You quickly put that aside, thinking that you will be a full-fledged princess, with all the duties, and you will have to leave Stardark to another anyway . . . and you know that dark and lively Shana will be a perfect companion to the horse.

The two of you find the Garden soon, encircled by broken-down walls of gray stone. Its interior is a riot of color, with flowering trees, rows of strange herbs, and flowers cresting the ground. And in the center an emerald dragon lies curled about a fabulous rose tree, with roses darker than night.

"That's it," Neal whispers in your ear.

"And the dragon is sleeping." You have a plan, as the two of you slide off Stardark's back, but before you can say anything, Neal says, "I've got an idea."

He examines his fishing pole. "I'm a pretty good caster. I think I can snag a rose off that tree without waking the beast."

You blink, surprised. "Well, I was just going to sneak in."

He shrugs. "Might work, might not."

"Well, the same goes for your idea."

He doesn't seem to recognize the insult in your voice. He shrugs, finally. "It's your choice, your highness."

And it is. But which seems best?

1. If you use your idea, turn to Pathway 38 (page 149).

2. If you use Neal's, go to Pathway 41 (page 158).

PATHWAY 34

"A bird in the hand is worth two in the bush," you mutter to yourself. "Even if I have to steal that bird first!"

Quietly, as silent as the desert lions were, you make your way down the slope. Small stones skitter away, rolling down the hill, and you hold your breath, but you might as well not worry. The ogres are now arguing so loudly over who won the last toss that a giant could come skipping up to them and they'd never hear it.

Nonetheless, you think that your pounding heart must be making almost as much noise as a giant as you crouch behind the tent and reach for the plump water bags. You grasp the heavy bags, lug them to rest over your shoulders, and turn to bolt.

"Drop it!" a gruff voice says, and you halt in your tracks, your heart pounding like a kettledrum.

"Will not," says a second. "It's my pot, and you lost—so there."

There is a curse and a grunt, and you realize the ogres are thumping each other.

You take a deep breath and run back up the slope, sure now that the ogres will never spot you.

But as you top the ridge, Stardark throws his head up from the other side. He spots you and smells the water you're carrying, and his stallion voice trumpets into the still air.

You don't look back as an angry shout rings out, and then another.

"There she is!"

Oh, Stardark, Stardark! But you can't blame him for the joy with which he greets you, nuzzling your hands eagerly as you tumble down the slope and fumble to loosen his reins. You let him have a quick handful of water, scarcely enough to wet his soft muzzle, before slinging the packs over the saddle and leading him to a rock so that you can climb on.

The ogre's minions are swarming over the ridge like angry bees, shouting and brandishing their weapons at you, their lean and hungry horses leaping over rocks and stones as they skitter down. Stardark bolts as you set your heels to his flanks, praying that there is enough speed left in him to take you away once more.

You head the black stallion toward the flatland, avoiding the gullies, which can lead blindly to dead ends, and staying away from the rough trail you just traveled. The horse picks his way out, and soon you are thundering over grass-packed plains, the dense blades flattened under his pounding hooves.

The ogres whoop with savage joy, whipping their mounts, hot on your heels. It's not fair! While you've been riding hard, their horses have been tethered and watered, resting for your appearance. You wrap your hand in his thick mane.

"Run, Star! Run!"

The horse gathers his muscles, his nostrils cupped wine-red to suck in the hot air, his neck foaming with his efforts. Surely nothing and no one can ever catch up with you now!

But as you look over your shoulder, you see the three dark riders close at hand. One of them carries a rope in his clawed hand. All he has to do is get close enough to throw it.

As your proud stallion falters, a keen whistle cuts across your fears, and a fifth horse pounds across the plains, a lean figure hunched close across his neck.

The rider draws close to you, reaching out, and you glimpse an intense face framed by blue-black hair tied back with a leather thong, dressed in buckskins. A nomad!

His hand grasps for you, and Stardark shies away in fear.

"Come to me," he calls, as the two desert horses race side by side. "My horse is fresh and can carry two . . . yours must run free if he's to stay on his feet!"

And, indeed, Stardark is faltering under you. You tear your hand from his whipping black mane and reach out for the young nomad warrior grasping for you. His hand and then his iron-hard arm wraps about you, sweeping you from the saddle.

You gasp as he slings you across the front of his flame-red horse. Out of desperation to stay on, you wrap both your hands in the stallion's mane as the nomad reins his horse away.

Stardark gathers himself bravely, his burden lessened, and follows.

The ogre soldiers are left behind as the young man tightens an arm about you, keeping you crushed to his body. The two of you outrun Rastik's minions.

Leagues later, the soldiers are no more to be seen, and the afternoon sun is dipping low on the horizon. The flame-colored chestnut has slowed to an easy lope, with which Stardark keeps pace, but the nomad's arm is no looser about your waist as you approach his camp.

He has said not a word, but you are terribly aware that he is a proud young man, a warrior, for his lance is sheathed by your slippered feet, and his bared arms are battle-scarred. You have gotten used to his scent of buckskins, campfire smoke, horses, and an herb you don't recognize. You hope that he hasn't been able to feel your heart still beating rapidly under your ribs, as you catch your breath.

Tall, dark-eyed men, strong and wiry, run out to meet the two of you, their colorful garb of silks and skins just as you remember. The tallest catches you as the rider slides you down from his mount, and you gasp in surprise.

The man sets you down with a laugh.

"Strange rabbit this is, Garon."

The boy, nearly man, laughs. "Indeed. I sprang her from a snare sent by ogres—some of Rastik's horse soldiers, by the looks of them."

The tall man stops laughing suddenly, and anger glints off his weathered face. He snaps his fingers.

A party of four men quickly gets together and leaves, without another word.

You catch Stardark's reins and stand quietly with him, stroking his wet neck.

The nomad prince talks quietly with the tallest man for a moment, his father or leader or both, and then turns to you. A smile lights up his face, accenting the high cheekbones and setting a gleaming in his wide, dark eyes. "We will have your stallion attended to, for he must be cooled and his legs seen to, and then watered and grained. You must be Princess Sarah of Marcelayne, for we recognize the stallion Stardark, once of our herds and given to her hand. You have done well with him."

High praise from a somber people. You smile as a young slip of a boy takes the reins from your hands and disappears with Stardark in the direction of a milling herd of horses.

You follow Garon to the tents and wagons, feeling strangely quiet. Rather than tell your story a hundred times over, you decide to keep your peace until Garon and the tall nomad can gather together their people to hear your tale. Garon stops beside a huge basin carved from cool green rock, its depths belled out to hold glistening water.

He gives you a dipper of water, which you gulp down thirstily, but he does not refill the dipper. You lick your lips, reminding yourself that every drop is precious here. Then he moistens a cloth and hands it to you, and you wash your hands and face, though you would gladly jump into the water cairn feet first and take a bath!

When you have finished, a circle of men and women are seated awaiting you. Garon sits down next to you and says gravely, "This is Princess Sarah of Marcelayne, whom I rescued not many leagues from here as she was hunted by three of Rastik's men."

What cool confidence this boy radiates! He's never bothered to ask if you are truly Sarah, or if you needed rescuing! Your face flushes as he pauses, and you realize others are waiting to hear you.

"Rastik, the ogrelord, captured my father and mother this morning. His troops hold my city."

A woman with a red paint design on one cheek, her gray-streaked hair plaited down to her waist, says, "Have you fled—or are you seeking us?"

"Neither. I—I took a pledge to win a race to free them . . . but your aid would be greatly appreciated."

"What is this race?"

You swallow. Your legs and back ache, and your tongue is still dry, making it hard to speak. "I must go to the Garden of Galatea and bring back an unwilted rose within three days."

A murmur runs through the circle. The tall man stirs. "You are taking the longest road to Galatea."

You meet his brown eyes. "I hoped to find friends along the way."

"Perhaps enough friends that you might bring back an army instead of a rose?"

Your ears buzz. You look about them . . . a simple people, without armor or swords, their children playing about the wagons and in the shadow, a stone's throw from you. How can you ask them to go to war for you?

"My father and I are sworn allies," says Garon. "Ask of us, and we will give you whatever we can!"

His voice sends a thrill through your body. You remember the strong grip of his arm about you, an embrace that sent your body racing into strange emotions. You are drawn to this young man, and you don't know what to do about it.

Continue the race or ask for an army? You duck your head and stare at your battered slippers, your feet curled under you. What will you say?

1. *If you ask the nomads to fight for your kingdom, your destiny lies in Pathway 6 (page 35).*
2. *If you ask them to help you win the race, your fate is told in Pathway 10 (page 47).*

PATHWAY
35

You swallow your tears. "Tyrone told me to go . . . and if he is lost, then he lost all helping me. I . . . I guess I must go on."

"Then go," roars the dragon, and frightened, you turn and run for your life. You mount Stardark, who rears in panic and takes to his heels, as the dragon bounds after you.

How the stallion finds the twisting road by the swamps, you'll never know, but find it he does, and past the swamps you flee, with the dragon winging ever overhead, bellowing and hissing at you like some frightful beast, which, of course, it is. It toyed with you in the Garden, you know, and your heart pounds in your chest as Stardark's hooves drum on the ground.

It is a lathered and nearly windbroken Stardark that staggers into Marcelayne, just a length ahead of the dragon. Ogre soldiers cry out and run in fear as its emerald shape swoops down over the city. Just as you reach the steps and your stallion lurches to a halt, the dragon hovers down close enough for you to hear its honeyed voice.

"I gave your horse the wings it needed to carry you home. No need to thank me, my dear. Your race is won."

And even if it hadn't been, the sight of the dragon is enough to send Rastik packing for the gate, followed hastily by his van of warriors.

THE END

PATHWAY
36

Quickly, you turn Stardark and kick him into a run, into the end of the valley that is heavily shrubbed and treed. You tether the stallion and climb down, to find yourself shaking in every limb, with fear and exhaustion. As you collapse upon a mossy bank, the horse puts his head down and calmly begins to tug at the tender shoots of grass, as though a dragon had not just faced him nearly head to head.

But how are you to know when it will be safe to approach the Garden of Galatea again, if ever? You eye the tree stretching overhead. If you were Shana, you'd have no trouble at all shinnying up that tree and taking a look. Well, you're not your bold and wonderful sister—but you can try to imitate her. With a sigh, you tug your skirts up and tuck them in at the waist, so that you can climb the tree.

After slips and scratches and prickles from a reluctant tree, you perch in one of its branches, thinking that you must look like a very large and very pink squirrel. Still, you can see the Garden from here, and the dragon paces its interior restlessly, watching over its domain.

You fall asleep waiting for the dragon to calm, and when you wake, you grab in panic at the tree branch, for you nearly plunge headfirst from the branch. As you right yourself, thrashing and cursing, Stardark lifts his head and whickers at you.

"No, I'm not all right! And I hope you're satisfied," you tell the horse. He wrinkles his muzzle at you.

As you squint to see more clearly, you can tell the reptile form has, at last, fallen quiet and curled itself about one of the trees of the garden. This may be your one and only chance, for shadows are lengthening across the valley and you have little time left. You must hurry!

Leaving Stardark in the grove, you creep over the fields and reach the broken stone wall. As you hug the cold gray surface, you are aware that you can hear nothing . . . not even a low snoring. Cautiously, you straighten to look over the wall—

And find yourself eye to eye with the dragon as it snorts in amusement!

"Ah, little worm . . . or should I say little cat, for your curiosity has caught you!"

Quickly, you look away from the golden jewel of eyes twinkling at you, wondering why it hasn't blasted you in your tracks.

The dragon rears up, resting its forearms on the wall. "A flower, is it? Or an herb? Who has sent you here to plunder my beautiful garden?"

141

"Actually, the garden isn't so beautiful," you blurt out, without thinking.

The dragon bristles. Its spines rattle, and its emerald hide fairly shines in indignation. "What's that?"

"Well, I mean . . . it's just that the wall is tumbling down, and your herbs . . . very nice, but they could use weeding. And your trees need pruning a little, too."

The dragon looks over his winged shoulder as if to consider your remark. Then it sighs. "You're right, of course. But I haven't the hands to work it, and slaves are hard to come by. Still and all, you're here, and I seem to have captured you."

"No, you haven't!" You stand up straight. "I've come to trade with you."

"Trade?"

"Yes. A week's worth of labor for a rose, a black one."

"I suppose you want to take the rose back first. They always do." The green beast sniffs in disdain.

"Well . . . I have to. I'm in this race, you see."

"Naturally." The dragon examines its claws. "Not good enough, though I'll admit I'm interested, and my garden does need working. How will you pledge yourself?"

You can breathe easier now that it appears the beast isn't going to blast you and, in fact, seems rather amiable. "I'll—I'll tell you where I live, and if I'm not back in a week, you can come fire the place."

"Hmmmmmmm." The dragon chews on one of

its claw tips. "Tell you what. It's a deal, but only if you can answer a riddle as well. It's in the dragon code that you must either defeat me or outwit me to get the best of me. I can't have other dragons thinking I let you plunder my garden just because I need help weeding!"

Your heart sinks. You've never been good at riddles, but you can't think of what else to do. "All right," you agree reluctantly.

The reptilian face smirks a little as it says, "All right. Here goes:

> "Once told, true.
> Twice told, broken.
> Third time for all,
> a rumor badly spoken.
> What am I?"

The dragon clears its throat. "That's a nice one, if I do say so myself."

Thoughts whirl in your head, like dust clouds from crossing the Elash. You can't remember any of the riddles you knew when you were young, except one about an egg, and you pull at the frayed waistband of your dress. Bother.

The dragon makes itself comfortable leaning on the wall. "Plenty of time. You have as long as you want to answer, unless I get hungry, that is."

You shudder. He nags at you as badly as Shana does when you know a secret and she wants you to tell it to her. Something clunks to a halt in your wild thoughts. A secret . . . that might be it. If

143

you tell one person, it's a secret, but two, it's not a secret any longer . . . and if you pass it along, it becomes ugly gossip. "A secret," you cry in triumph. "Your answer is a secret!"

The dragon bows its head in defeat. "Take your rose, my dear, and remember your promise to return."

"Oh, I will, I will!" And if Rastik doesn't stand by his vow, you will have an angry green dragon buzzing around the castle like a hornet! "Come to the castle in Marcelayne if I'm not back."

As you whistle for Stardark, the black stallion races up, ears pricking and snorting at the sight of the dragon leaning on the wall. But you mount him quickly and set his flying hooves back on the path to your kingdom, the black rose clutched triumphantly in your hand.

The desert riders of the Elash are there to meet you, and they whoop in triumph as you crest the border. Garon rides out to join you, and your two stallions, black and red, flash across the sands, tireless as the wind.

He reins away at the far side of the Elash, having guided you through shortcuts. His last act is to give you a torch so that you may ride through the night.

"We're on the far side of Marcelayne," he tells you, "so you have most of the night ahead of you. Ride slowly, but safely, and dawn will greet your victorious entry into the city."

"Thank you," you murmur, and the bold nomad prince leans from his horse and steals a kiss.

"Nothing less!" he laughs at you. "Tell your father we must be closer allies! I will come treatying for that."

"And I will welcome you," you answer, your pulse pounding.

The orange flame of the torch guides you through the green tracks of Marcelayne, and true to Garon's word, you enter through the gates of the city at dawn, the sky blazing pink and orange at your back.

Stardark's hooves ring out on the paved road, and curious townspeople peer out of their windows, wary of what Rastik and his army may be doing now. But as they see you, shouts of joy follow you down the street.

Thus it is that Rastik knows you've won before you reach the courtyard and the palace steps, and he is waiting there to meet you, a curious expression on his ogrish face.

You hand him the rose, and he crushes it angrily and waves to his men. "Retreat, and leave the city." He rips the shackles from your father as one of his lieutenants unchains your mother and Shana.

"You haven't heard the last of me, Joseph," the ogre overlord swears, as he mounts his scrawny horse and raises a mailed fist.

Your father hugs you in joy as the invaders leave the city, but you notice your father's worried frown.

You smile. "I wouldn't worry about Rastik too much, Father."

"And why is that?" he asks wearily.

A blush colors your face as you answer, "I think we've made some very strong allies with the Elash riders!"

THIS IS THE END OF THIS ADVENTURE.

PATHWAY 37

"I'm sorry, sir dragon, but I've met many creatures on this race of mine, some with honor and some without. I will trade whatever I can for passage into the garden," you answer, knowing that the dragon will stick to a bargain if it makes one.

The beast chews thoughtfully on a claw tip. "Partial I am to gold," it says.

"I have none."

"Your hair is gold."

You sigh, for your waist-length hair is your pride . . . but then, there is little else you have given up these past two days. You have nothing to cut it with, but you lean over from the saddle and twist your hair into a golden rope. "Then it is yours, sir dragon, if you can free it from my head."

The jaws snap, and the heavy length of hair is shorn from your head at the nape of your neck. You shudder as you realize how close you came to having your head snapped off instead.

The dragon tucks the length of hair under one

arm. "One item may you take from the garden," it says and leans back to watch you enter.

You pick the rose and give your thanks, but winning the object does not fill you with joy. You have given this race everything you had to give—your youth, your beauty, even your first love.

You can only pray it will be enough as you take up the reins to return home to free your family.

THIS IS THE END OF YOUR ADVENTURE.

PATHWAY
38

You sniff. "Undoubtedly you think you can do it. Well, I think you can't, and it's harebrained. Fish a rose off the tree, indeed! You hold Stardark and wait for me."

Neal gets out a "But" before you've hiked up your torn and dirty petticoats and stepped into the garden.

Each step is a quiet movement, as you remember all that your father's huntsmen have told you about stealth. Twigs bend but don't break under your light weight, and your eyes are on the rising and falling flanks of the sleeping beast.

What a dragon! It must wrap three times about the trunk of the tree, its claws sharp as a dagger, and its scales gleaming like green enamel. Any knight would fear to approach it, yet here you are, tiptoeing across the garden, hoping those eyelids stay tightly shut.

You're almost there, so close you can stand and reach, and your hand is brushing the tree limb when a honeyed voice says, "What, thief, are you doing?"

You gasp, as the dragon's head rears level with yours. "I—I, ah, I—"

You can hear Neal vaulting the stone wall to help you, but the dragon says, "Never mind. A black rose you want, and it's a black rose you'll be," and suddenly, the world feels very queer, as you have a shrinking feeling, and your legs feel glued to the ground.

Neal roars, "You'll never get away with this!" as he swoops you up and carries you off, the dragon blasting fire at his heels in anger. He jumps Stardark, and the two of you thunder off, the disgruntled dragon hissing in anger.

But—but this is all wrong. You can't speak, and Neal cups you in his hands. His face looks at you tenderly.

"A rose," he whispers. "The dragon's turned you into a rose."

But you're still you! Thoughts reel in your head, and for a long moment, you faint away. Time passes oddly for a flower, for when you awaken, you are cuddled gently in the palm of Neal's hand, and you can look out over the crest of Stardark, as he dismounts, still carrying you gently.

Rastik's face looms over you, and you shake, your petals rustling with a silken noise, as he snarls.

"The bet was with the girl!"

Neal stands steadfastly. "The bet was that the horse could run fast enough to bring back a rose before it wilts, and here it is."

You can feel the anger coursing through the boy's body. "I warn you, Rastik, to stand by your bet, for the horse has done all asked of it, and more—and we came home by way of the Elash desert, where the nomad nation stands ready to war with you, if need be."

The ogre snarls angrily and snaps his head back. "Then I shall leave—but once again, King Joseph, I swear to return."

"At your peril," you hear your father warn.

In moments, you are cradled in the soft hand of your mother as Neal says, "This rose is your daughter Sarah. I'm sorry. I don't know what can be done."

Shana's sparkling eyes look down at you as she says with delight, "Why—that means another quest—to disenchant Sarah!"

THE END OF ONE ADVENTURE AND THE BEGINNING OF ANOTHER

PATHWAY 39

As you turn Stardark down the road to the swamps, the brush rattles and figures launch themselves at you, grabbing at Stardark's reins, and a third ogre hangs on to the stallion's tail, as he neighs angrily and kicks out.

But it is too late . . . you're captured.

Yellow tusks gleam as the soldier nearest you grins in triumph. "Rastik never loses!" he says, as he mounts his horse and takes you prisoner.

You put your chin up as they turn Stardark toward home. "Maybe this time," you mutter, but your mind is eagerly racing toward home and your family. Rastik may have won this bet, but you know when you put your head together with your sister Shana, you will be able to come up with a better scheme! You will never rest until your family and your home is freed.

THE END OF THIS PATHWAY

PATHWAY 40

With a shiver, you face the proud nomad boy and his flaming stallion.

"I have to do what I have to do," you say. "I vowed to run a race, and now that's ended. But I can't do anything else, any more than—than you would waste water."

His sharp eyes look deep into yours, and then he nods abruptly. "Then Arrow will bear your weight with mine once more. Let me carry you to the borders of your country."

He leans down and swings you easily onto his mount, and you are once more riding in front of him, one of his strong arms clasped about your waist.

The Elash nomads know of many ways to cross the desert, you discover, as by nightfall you are approaching the city gates, leagues cut off your journey by Garon's wily knowledge. If only you had had such knowledge when you made your pledge.

Garon loosens you and lets you dismount, but

his arm lingers about you longer than necessary. For hours you have been aware of the strength of his young body next to yours, and the intelligence of his eyes, and the gentleness of his hands and voice, especially as he urged the injured Stardark to keep up with you.

"Remember the poison," he whispers to you as he leans down now. "And, failing that, I will bring back an army to free you, if it takes all my life."

You gasp, startled, as he steals a kiss and then whirls his horse in the night and disappears in the shadows. Ogre guards call out, "Who goes there?"

Your last few steps of the journey made miserable by jeering guards, you lead Stardark up the lane of the city toward the castle front steps and courtyard. It is packed with ogre soldiers, horrible by day and more grotesque by torchlight, their tusks gleaming as they laugh and howl at your failure.

Rastik himself appears on the steps.

"What? Back so soon?"

You lift your chin. "My horse is lamed."

"Ah. The fortunes of the game, my dear. Well, you have lost and I am the victor. Bride cups," he bellows over his shoulder at a fat and warty soldier. "Bring me the bride cups so that I may drink to my betrothal."

You shudder, but force a smile. "If I may fetch them, your lordship . . . as the first of my many duties as your chattel."

The ogrelord looks at you in surprise, then lets out a howl of a laugh and waves you by, to find the silver cups rolling in the looted kitchen.

But you waste no time emptying the contents of Garon's pouch into one of the cups.

Your family awaits you as well when you return to Rastik, the cups brimming with red wine. Their faces are hollow, for they've had little sleep and much ill treatment. Only Shana shows a spark of life.

"Sarah! Did you win already?"

"No." You shake your head sadly at her. "I'm sorry. Stardark fell crossing the Flash . . . twisted his leg. I had no choice but to return."

Your father says nothing, but tightens his jaws as you turn and offer a cup to Rastik.

"My ogrelord," you murmur and drop your eyes as befits an engaged girl.

His thorny hand takes the cup and wafts it high, so that all his men assembled in the courtyard may see it.

"I have won the wager. We will have a wedding tomorrow . . . and afterward, kill all the royal family but my new bride!"

You gasp, as your mother faints and the king catches her, and Shana lets out a wail of fright. "But you promised!"

Rastik only roars with crude laughter, then drowns his voice with the contents of the silver cup. You pour your wine out over the steps as he finishes, for now you know you have done the right thing. Garon was right!

The ogrelord growls. "Fill the cup and drink it, girl—you have no choice!"

"I have every choice. It is you, Rastik, who have none!"

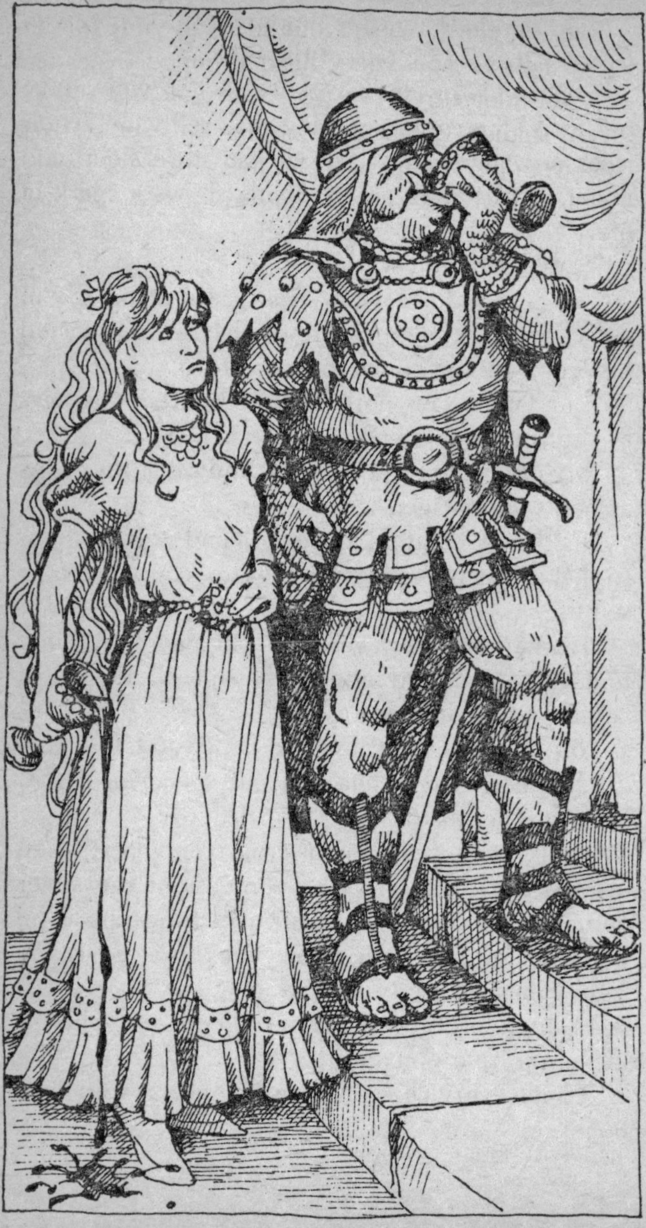

The ogrelord reaches out to seize you, but instead falls to one knee, head drooped over, and lets out a loud snore.

His soldiers stand bewildered as you tear the key ring from his leather belt and toss it to your father.

Rastik wakes suddenly, and mumbles. His reddish eyes focus on you. "What—what have you done?"

"Only a minor poison, Rastik—but one which you dare not ignore! I gave you the sleeping poison, and its antidote is the small sunflower which grows many leagues from here in the full of the moon. If you hurry, you just might reach the isle of Borik to harvest the flower before sleep takes you permanently!"

Rastik stumbles to his feet with a roar of rage and cries out, "Disperse, you men! And hurry . . . there is no time to (yawn) waste!"

The ogres run to do their master's bidding, and in a moment or two, after another short nap, Rastik leads his army from your father's gates.

With whoops of joy they surround you, and your face runs wet with tears of happiness.

But your father says gently, "How did you know of such a thing, Sarah?"

"I had a little help from a friend, who, if I'm very lucky, will come back soon. At least, I hope he will." And you and Stardark both look across the courtyard, down the lane and to the city gates, where beyond lie the borders of other lands . . . and other hearts.

THE END

PATHWAY
41

For a moment you stand there, every bit the miffed princess, and then you relax. How stupid to quarrel over this, when everything that can help should be used.

You nod. "Why don't you try first, Neal, for that will surely not wake the dragon, even if it fails. If it does, then I shall have to try to sneak in."

"Done." Neal's blue-green eyes sparkle, and the early-morning sun fairly sets his hair aglow as he bends over his fishing pole, long fingers worrying at the line. Finally he says, "I think I have it now." He pulls a hook off his vest and replaces the other. "This is my lucky hand-tied fly. My uncle, the duke, tied it for me."

He doesn't see your mouth gape open as he turns to cast the hook. The line flies through the air with a whip of his wrist, and just then you remember where you have seen red-gold hair like that before—a friend of your father's, a king from far away, with sons—and you narrow your eyes in suspicion.

The hook falls short and lands atop the dragon, and Neal sucks in his breath as he draws it back, the hook making no impression at all on the hide of armor the dragon wears.

A second time the hook and line whips through the air, to snag at the base of a tightly closed bud. You hold your breath, unwilling to say anything now, not until he gets that rose. . . .

Neal snaps his wrist, and the bud rips from the tree, flying through the air above your heads. He drops the pole in triumph and gathers up the rose.

You watch as he drops the basket and pole and says, "Shall we head for the castle?"

"And how do you suggest we do that, *Prince* Neal?" you ask sweetly.

He blushes, which makes his freckles stand out, as he looks at you. "Not in front of the dragon," he answers, as he hoists you aboard Stardark. "There's time enough for all that later."

"But," you point out, "as a poor fisherboy, aren't you leaving behind the equipment you need to earn your livelihood?"

His face becomes white as the dragon whuffles, and he vaults on behind you, saying tensely, "Later."

Much later, you have forgotten your anger, as his arms are tight about you, and the leagues behind you, the black rose safely gotten, as he tells you a story of a princeling who fell in love with a miniature painting of a young princess, and came in disguise to see if she would accept the idea of a suitor.

As he finishes his story, you say nothing, but a smile uplifts the corners of your mouth.

"Well?"

You look over your shoulder at him. "Well, what?"

"Well, would you?"

"That all depends. First I have to get rid of Rastik."

"And then?"

"Then I'd have to meet the princeling."

Neal leans his face close, and your lips touch, not by accident. "Consider him met, Sarah," he says softly, and the journey home passes by far quicker than the journey to get the black rose.

THE END

PATHWAY 42

"I have until tomorrow evening," you answer, "and if I can save Tyrone today . . ."

"Done," hisses the dragon. He cracks his claw knuckles. "I'm pleased you asked, actually. I haven't been goblin-roasting in a long time. Now, let me see . . . under that mountain, is it?"

You look over your shoulder. "Yes, that's it."

The dragon frowns, or seems to, green scales rubbing against one another. "Those tunnels are a bit small for me, but there's another entrance. Follow me, and don't dawdle."

It's all you can do to knee Stardark after the beast once you regain the saddle, for the horse is wary of the great reptile, and you can't blame him. But the dragon awaits you at the mountainside, and rips away a great boulder.

The creature grins, red tongue lolling through ivory fangs. "This pebble was once placed here to keep me out. Can you imagine?"

Frankly, you can't, after seeing the ease with which the rock is turned aside. You follow the dragon into a great cavern, which echoes with goblin shout and elfin cry.

As you and the dragon plunge forward, you see a host of goblins struggling with a host of elves, and Tyrone is at their fore. Your heart leaps to see the blood streaking his fair head, but his sword blade still takes a heavy toll of the enemy.

With a snort and a bellow, the dragon plunges into the fray, stomping and sizzling whatever he can, and the goblins soon turn and run into the tunnels for their lives.

The elves let out a cry of triumph as the dragon swallows the last goblin up, after neatly roasting him first.

Tyrone snatches you up and gives you a hug. "Bless you for bringing him back with you," the elf prince says, and seals his gratitude with a kiss. He then turns triumphantly to the army gathered in the great cavern.

"We owe our lives to this girl . . . can we give her back any less?"

"No!" thunders back the cry.

"Then this day we march on Rastik, and free Marcelayne."

"Free, free, free!" echoes the shout, and Tyrone replaces you on Stardark to lead you from the mountain, as he smiles and adds, "Remember that you are loved."

You look at him, and know the warmth of that feeling. "As if a girl could ever forget an elf kissed her!"

THE END

PATHWAY 43

You wiggle down from Garon's embrace, calling, "Star, Star," gently, the way you did when he was a wild foal, a suckling, and feared you.

The black stallion's head moves slightly, and a soft brown eye regards you, before his ears flick forward again and he watches the sweep of horses running past.

"Let him go," Garon says quietly.

"I can't! I can't! Suppose he can't keep up with the herd. There are desert lions and—and all sorts of things. And I love him."

You reach Stardark's side now and grasp the bridle, pulling the stallion's head down to you, and stroke his forelock until the thunder of the wild horses is long past. Then you lead the animal up the slope to where Garon sits waiting for you, a peculiar look on his face.

"Because you love him," the boy says, "you do not let him go."

You smile, and it quivers in the corners, because you are so near to crying. You wanted to give Stardark his heart's desire. "Maybe when he is healed and I know—I know he can survive here."

Garon says nothing else, but dismounts from Arrow. The two stallions eye each other warily as the two of you walk down the slope.

"There! There is the Garden of Galatea."

A faint tinge of green spreads from your feet, growing down the far slope, until it becomes a lush green carpet in a tiny valley more than a league from you, a valley boxed on two sides by mountains and a third by a thick grove of trees, which eventually give way to the Manofee Hole, the Swamps of Despairing.

The horses lift their heads and push the two of you down the slope, faster, for the scent of fresh, clean water is in the air.

Still, the sun is hot on your brows and your feet sore by the time you reach the walled Garden. The gray stones are piled, neat and orderly, in a circle about the rows of herbs and flowers and a grove of trees, each different in a splendid way.

You find yourself holding your breath without knowing why. Garon stirs.

"I'm glad," he says finally, "that I came with you."

"So am I," you answer, and then add with a voice you're not sure is yours, "I think I love you."

Before the nomad prince can answer, a green-and-brown shadow darts from behind a tree.

"Beware! The dragon awakes!"

A shuddering of leaves cascades about the wood nymph as a huge green reptilian tail lashes out and encircles her. She screams as the dragon imprisons her and lunges his serpentine bulk at the two of you.

Garon frees his sword from its sheath, but Stardark trumpets a warning and leaps the walls without hesitation, sailing through the air like a dark bolt of lightning as you cry out, "Star! No!"

For the stallion has always hated snakes, with a vengeance, and has trampled more than one of them to protect you. He plunges, rearing and pawing, at the dragon with another trumpeting neigh.

The dragon's crimson tongue flickers as the emerald jaws open and steam issues forth. You grab Garon's arm.

"He'll be scorched to death! Do something!"

But before either of you can move, the stallion stomps downward, ebony legs flashing and kicking. The dragon's jaws clash in midair, and his forelegs grasp the horse's flanks, clawing and opening up huge crimson welts. The saddle falls away useless in shreds. The stallion bucks and rears again, striking. Ichor gushes out from the dragon's head, and the beast collapses on the garden bed.

Stardark screams angrily a third time, and his sharp hooves cut the dead dragon to bits.

The wood nymph shrugs free from the relaxing coils of the beast's tail and runs lightly toward you, as Stardark backs away, snorting. Then he throws his head up and lets his stallion challenge ring across the valley.

Garon helps you over the garden wall as the nymph holds out her hands in welcome.

"Thank you, thank you, mortals all, who saved me." She is pretty in an unearthly way, and for a moment you are jealous of Garon's eyes upon her. That moment is gone in a flash, as you see Stardark trembling in shock, from the poison in the dragon's claws.

"Star!" You throw your arms about his neck.

The nymph laughs. "Fear not. I have something that can save him, and even improve him a little."

She picks a flower, a strange flower, and smashes it between her greenish hands, staining them with a purple fluid. This she rubs along the crimson slashes on the horse's flanks, and even down the right foreleg, which Stardark is favoring a little.

The wounds open up, and a white pus gushes out, the dragon's poison, you think. You shudder as the stallion twists his neck and nickers in pain, pushing at you to help him.

But the white is not poison. It unfolds and furls, and then darkens to charcoal . . . as two graceful, swanlike wings blossom from Stardark's former wounds. A Pegasus! The nymph has made a Pegasus of the black stallion.

And now your race is truly won. You pick a black rose quickly from the tree bearing them and say to the nymph, "This is all I need."

You mount Stardark, knowing that the winged horse will be back in Marcelayne before dark, and your race of peril will be won a full day early.

The nymph fades into the shadows, humming a song of nonsense to her plants, as Garon holds his hand out to you.

"Take me with you."

Tears well up, and you blink rapidly. "No," you answer softly. "I can't. But in a few months hence, when my father calls for suitors, you're more than welcome to answer."

"But I thought you said you loved me."

"And because I do, I must leave you—for now."

You blow him a kiss, as Stardark flexes his wings and starts into a run across the garden, clearing the rock wall in a jump that never touches, for then the two of you are airborne, for home.

THIS IS THE END OF THIS ADVENTURE, FOR NOW.

PATHWAY 44

"**I** must have the rose!" you declare, and Neal swings his sword loose.

"Then I'll get it for you," the young man swears, and breaks clear of the mosses, attacking a firefly as it darts down at him.

The insect is a golden fury, as big as a small dog, with gauzy wings and a brilliance that blinds the eye. Sparks fly as the steel bites into it, and Neal cries in pain, as those sparks quickly eat into the shirt on his back, leaving red welts behind. You snap off a branch of the weeping tree surrounding you, a branch that fans out at the end, like a large swatter, determined not to let Neal face your task alone.

You join him, as a swarm of fireflies dart from the treetops, skimming the jewellike pond, their angry buzz making it impossible to even shout to one another.

Your fan works as well as his sword, and the air is splattered with a golden shower of sparks, as fireflies meet with one end or another. Then, just

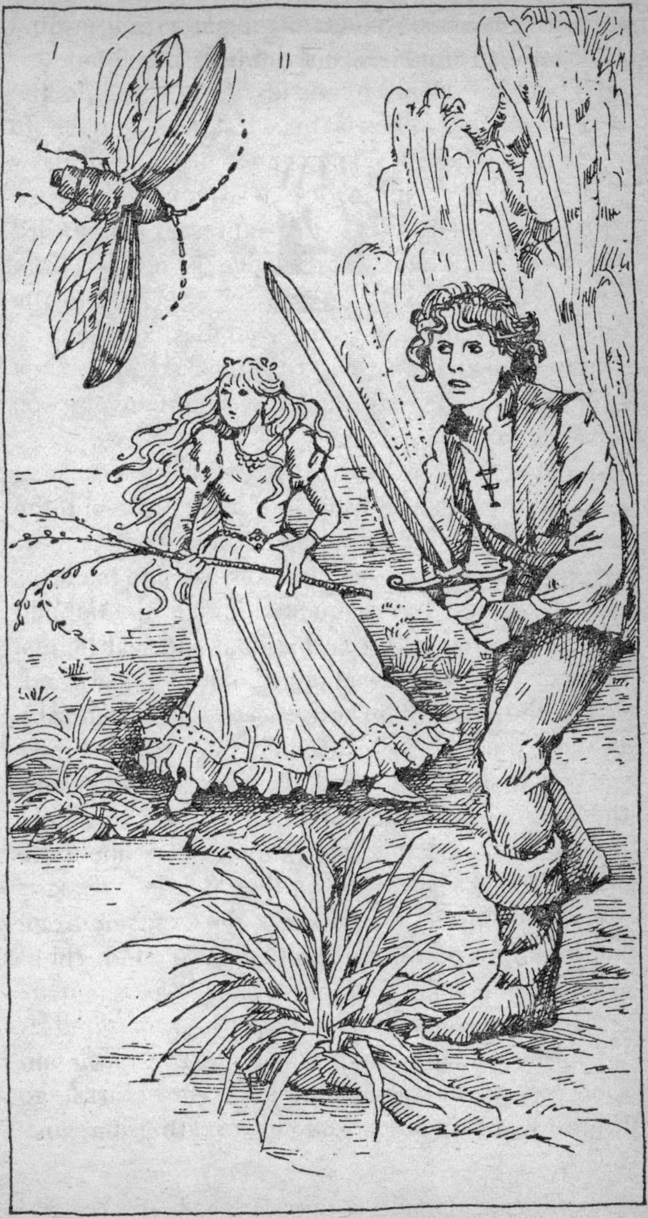

as suddenly, the sky is empty and the soft ground littered with the bodies of the insects.

"Quickly," Neal commands, as you run to the rose bush and pluck a bud just ripe enough to open into a flower. "The sounds of that will draw Rastik's soldiers, if they are near enough."

He holds Stardark's reins and tosses you aboard the saddle. "The swamp's edge is not far from here, and I will set you back on the road to the Elash. It's your only chance, for Rastik's men are bound to have the swamp road blocked, since they saw you ride in here, and the mountains are too treacherous."

Before you can protest at the sudden turn of events, the modest fisherboy has drawn out the method of your return like a field commander. True to his word, as you duck low-hanging branches and Stardark's hooves squelch through the bog, he breaks through into a clearing, and you see a weed-choked path ahead of you, out of the swamps.

"To the Elash," he orders, and slaps Stardark's rump.

"But what about you?" you ask, holding back the stallion's startled response.

A smile crosses his face. "Don't worry about me . . . but make sure my brother is safe," he says enigmatically, as you loosen the reins and let Stardark bolt across the ground, glad to be rid of the treacherous swamps.

You put Neal behind and out of your mind as the black stallion sets his heels to the road, and soon you are in the red desert wastelands of the Elash. A hot wind steals the breath from your mouth, and your sodden clothes almost sizzle dry. You slow the horse's pace, knowing that you have a full night of riding and perhaps more to break through, and the ground is not all smooth and sandy. Treacherous gullies break its surface, and jumbles of rocks, and scruffy-looking brush that rips at your skirt.

You give Stardark the bit as the sun dips low, and the leagues thunder away under his hooves, and the desert sun gives way to the moon, low and milky-white in the night. You stop once at a well, keeping Stardark from drinking his fill and foundering, letting the horse have only enough to keep him going, and even at that, you cannot let him run for a while.

As he paces you across the distance, you listen carefully to his breathing, ignoring your own stiff and bruised body, for your destiny now depends on his welfare.

Meanwhile, the rose in your hand opens to the desert heat. In the night you can scarcely see its petals, but as dawn lightens the sky, you see in dismay its wide-open face.

"Don't wilt," you cry in dismay, and when you stop at a second well, you carefully wrap the stem in a soaked rag from your dress, but your thought is too late. The flower is full open and not likely to last the day, especially as the wind sucks the very moisture from your own skin, and your lips are cracked and sore.

Will you make it in time to win the race?

Stardark whickers as you climb back in the saddle, and you let him have his way, knowing that only his speed can save you now.

There is no joy in you when at last his tired hooves thunder upon the paved lanes leading to the castle, and the ogre soldiers hold back cheering crowds, for though you have made it in time, the black rose has failed, and so have you.

Rastik awaits you on the steps, terrible in leather and studs, his brow glowering, as Stardark staggers to a halt and you all but fall off, nearly unable to stand.

Shana holds on to your mother's hand tightly as you lurch up the steps to the ogrelord and present your trophy—not wilted, but dried, dried as hard as the desert sands. Tears run down your face.

"The race is won," says Rastik, in an oddly sad manner. "But not won." He reaches out and grabs the rose.

As the dried petals crumble to dust in his warted fist, he throws back his head and gives out a cry of pain, a horrible cry of agony that shocks you, and you fall away from him. The very air ripples about him, and shudders, and then a curtain of darkness surrounds the ogrelord.

When it drops, a tall man stands there, his eyes glistening with tears.

"You've done it after all, Sarah!"

You blink, for the man might be the image of Neal, a decade yet to come. "But I—I don't understand."

The man stretches and laughs, as he orders the ogres to release your family. "I was enchanted by Rastik to be in his image, and only the black rose could break the enchantment. Rastik is under a spell of another's making and cannot leave the land of his exile, so your father had nothing to fear from him—but Rastik would have his revenge. My younger brother and I ventured too near . . . and I was caught. Neal followed me when I was sent here with an army, and he vowed to find a black rose himself to help. But when you offered a race, I had already found the information I needed when we plundered your library—begging pardon for my terrible manners, but you must remember I was Rastik in nearly every deed—and so I sent you instead."

"But Neal was the boy who helped me get the rose."

The man smiles kindly. "Then his efforts were not in vain, either."

Your father hugs you, as you feel faint. "We will have a feast," he declares, "as soon as we find Neal and bring him back."

You look around. "What about the ogres?"

The soldiers stand around in confusion, pig eyes blinking as though they can scarcely comprehend what is happening.

"I think," says the former ogrelord thoughtfully, "we will need a few more black roses. They used to be my captains."

Despite your father's embrace, you sit down suddenly on the steps, laughing. "Then I know where I can send you . . . but forgive me if I don't go myself, this time!"

Everyone laughs as Stardark puts in a loud whinny as though agreeing.

THIS IS THE END.

PATHWAY
45

You shake your head, trying to put aside the strange enchantment of the elf prince, for you feel his presence in your very bones. "I can't leave Stardark behind."

He bows again, gallantly. "Then I will aid you. Does he come to a whistle?"

"He does . . . but my voice will never carry that far."

"Sound the notes, if you will, and I will see if I can call the beast."

Your lips are dry, and you falter, then repeat the notes more clearly, though Tyrone winces mockingly.

"Never was a mortal who could match a songbird. Still, you have a pleasant enough voice. No doubt you can sing."

"No doubt," you say dryly, for you are considered quite a good singer in Marcelayne.

Tyrone laughs, then purses his lips and sounds the whistle, and it pierces the mountain air, straight as an arrow and strong as a staff, carrying, you think, to the far corners of the world.

He motions for you to be seated on a tree stump, then takes off his short cloak and settles it about your shoulders. "I will see that you are properly clothed when we reach my demesne. Elves forget that mortals have thin blood."

The warmth of the short cloak is like that of a fire, and you reply, "I don't think that we have thin blood—just that you carry a magic about within your cloaks."

Tyrone looks sharply at you, then laughs. "Perhaps. I had forgotten that, too."

The clop-clop of hooves striking interrupts you, and soon the mountain pass is filled with the dark form of Stardark, answering his whistle. You jump up happily, for the stallion looks none the worse, as you stroke his legs to see if he has injured himself at all.

Strong and clean, his skin dances under your touch, and you smile at him as he nips at your hair.

"A fine horse indeed. Now, perhaps, we will be on our way, and you will tell me how you came to be trespassing in our demesne."

Stardark follows behind happily, as the elf bows and points out a trail to you, through a thicket of pine boughs and cones that you had not seen before and probably never would have, had not one of the elves led you to it.

"I wasn't trespassing without need," you say to Tyrone, who perks a tipped ear to hear you better. "Rastik has returned, and invaded my father's kingdom."

"Ah. Then you are looking for allies."

"Not really. I—ah—bet him the surrender of the kingdom against a task we would perform. A horserace, of a kind. My little sister thought of it, as Rastik is a gambler."

"And this race?"

"To go to the Garden of Galatea, find a black rose, and return it unwilted before three days pass."

Tyrone nods in appreciation. "That would prove a horse's mettle, indeed, though a faerie horse could do it with ease."

You bristle a little, to have Stardark thought of as a lesser being. "We were doing quite well until the worg-riding goblins attacked us."

Tyrone ignores the edge in your voice as he turns to eye Stardark. "He looks fit, for this being the second day upon the trail."

"First."

"First?" says the elf, considering, and an arched eyebrow goes higher. "Really?" He purses his lower lip and pulls on it in thought.

"An alliance is a serious thing, but you have reminded me that I am quite fond of mortals, indeed." He strokes your hair, sending a chill of pleasure down your back that surprises you. "And war is an even more serious thing. Show me that there is something worth fighting for—like the lineage of this beast, and a pretty smile from your lips. Give me a race against one of my horses. Win, and we'll help you."

You tilt your head. "Done," you say, before you quite realize what you've said, for you have no idea what the elf has in mind, but his mocking, dancing eyes hold yours again, and you feel your heart tumble in surprise.

Tyrone whistles again, and in the bat of an eye, a white horse appears upon the path, a dancing steed without rein or harness upon him, for he will suffer none. Tyrone leaps to his back, and you mount Stardark. You follow him to a crest, where a winding path leads down to a valley half hidden by purple shadows, for it is near night here, where the mountain cuts off the daylight early.

"To the edge of the demesne, and the first one to reach it is the winner."

You catch your breath. It is a hair-raising downhill path, one completely unfamiliar to you and Stardark. Still, you have agreed, and you desperately need the aid of the elves if you can get it. So thinking, you nod and gather the reins, then knot your hands in Stardark's thick mane.

With a shout, the two of you spring forward on your mounts, and the race is begun. Stardark flies across the ground, barely touching it with his hooves, but the elfin horse is ahead, and your black stallion but a dark shadow of his fleetness.

You close your eyes, the dizzying turns of the mountain path making you sick with fear, and you cannot help Stardark by guiding him at all, only by staying on and not falling off. Thus it is that when you open your eyes, you see the foot of the mountain path, and a crowd of cheering elves leaping up and down in front of you, and Star's bobbing head a muzzle, then a head, then a neck in front of the faerie horse!

Tyrone leans low over his mount's neck, whispering into the flicking ears of the white beast, and you lean low as Stardark stretches out, pulling ever farther and faster, on flat ground now, meadow grass cut to shreds by his streaking hooves.

"Run, Star!" you whisper, knowing he is running for the sheer joy of it, and you can get no more speed out of him than his bursting heart is already giving.

Home by half a length, you shoot past the crowd of elves and into the shadows of the houses, marvelous spiraling buildings of gold and silver that glitter in the twilight.

Tyrone jumps off his mount with a shout, his face lit in happiness.

"Well done, Sarah, well done! Your mount has feet of quicksilver, and a heart deeper than dwarven mines. You have good right to be proud of him. And yourself as well. I never thought to see a woman that could ride that path downward."

You shake your head as Tyrone helps you down. "I didn't ride him, he simply took whatever burdens were on his back, and we flew with him."

The elf prince smiles gently, as he turns to a girl standing behind him. "Evelynne, this is Princess Sarah, from Marcelayne. She's had a rough trip. Please help her bathe and change, for we will celebrate tonight!"

Without another word about helping you, he wheels and leaves, and you are helped into an elfin building by the girl, who frowns slightly, but soon the two of you are laughing, as she helps you find a dress to wear, and light, supple elfin boots that fit like gloves.

It is full dark when you emerge, and the village is light with glowing orbs of gold that give their soft color to the night. The lane is set with tables, and those tables heaped with food, as sleek hounds wind in and out of chairs and occupants, and elfin laughter makes music in the air.

Tyrone jumps up and sits you next to him. He whispers, "Eat quickly, for then we will dance."

"But my father—"

"Later," the elf prince says, as he presses a golden plate of food in front of you. "Your horse is stabled. Now tend to yourself, and I will tend to you!"

You are hungry, ravenous, you discover, for the elf food is light and hot, and yet when you have eaten a plateful, you feel almost as if you have eaten nothing at all. The drink he has given you is not a juice, but not a wine either, and its amber fire flows through you, so that when he gathers you up to dance, you practically float into his arms.

Never in all your dreams of elves could you have imagined the music that fills the air, and the joyous voices, and the whirling figures of elves that pass you, as Tyrone puts his arm about you and whirls you with them. Your heart beats so rapidly that you're sure he must hear it, and you wonder what it is you are feeling. Could it be—could it be love?

Hours later, a sliver of a moon holds the skies, and the elves are drifting off to the spiraling tow-

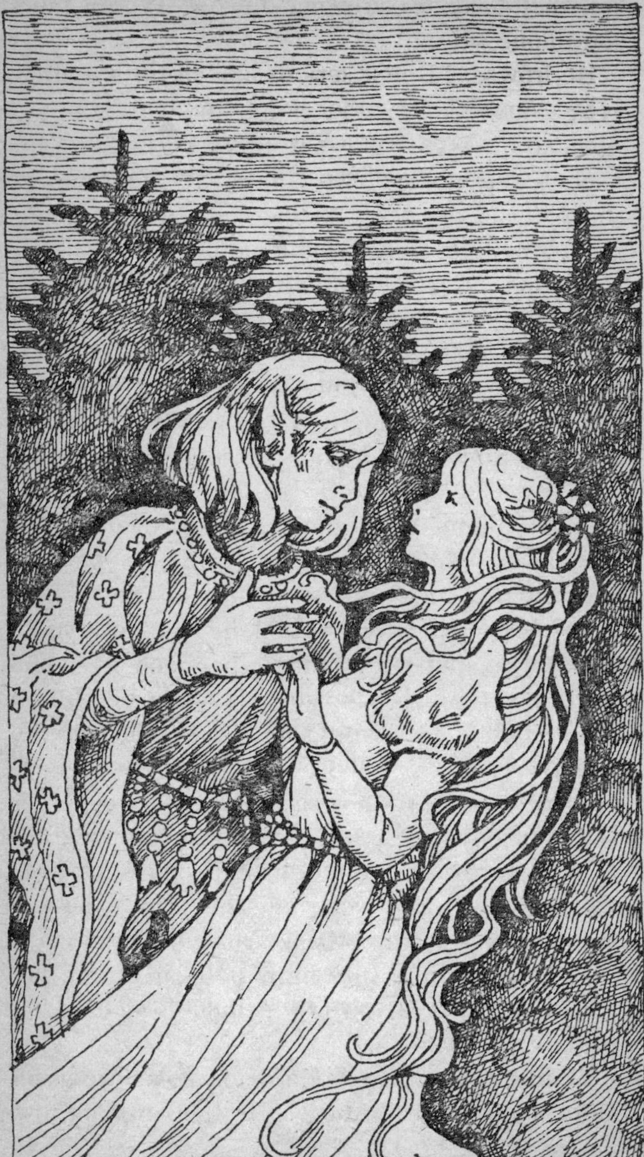

ers, their laughter growing dim, as Tyrone pulls you to one side.

He frowns, his first serious look of the evening. "The council won't go for it," he announces.

"Go for what?" you ask dreamily.

"For war against the ogrelord. I'm sorry, Sarah . . . I did my best."

"Why—why didn't you tell me, earlier?" His words now cut through your golden haze of emotions, and you blink in bewilderment.

"I couldn't. I wanted you to enjoy this evening, for I have a proposal, and it is a dire one. I wanted you to dance and laugh and sing a little first."

You shake your head and sit down on a fallen log. You notice the meadow is quiet and dewy, and darkening now as the fellowship of elves fades away. "What is it?"

"There is an underground tunnel. It will take us to the Garden of Galatea, for our people used to find our medicines there. It is treacherous and steep, and there is a possibility goblins have overrun it. But I can get you through and back before tomorrow night is ended, and from there you will have your race won."

Tunnels. Underground. Goblins. You shudder. That or go on by yourself, for your mind is clearing now.

Tyrone is watching you, waiting for your answer.

1. *If you go with him, turn to Pathway 24 (page 100).*

2. *But if you decide to go on your own, find Pathway 47 (page 184).*

PATHWAY 46

You place your hand over Eruman's. "Do whatever is necessary," you whisper hoarsely, sore afraid for your family.

The nomad leader nods briskly. "A wise decision, your highness. We will do as you command."

But Garon gives you a look of bitter hurt as he reins away his gray mare, and you realize that whatever might have been between the two of you is now gone, for you have rejected his idea.

You would call out after him, but your voice is dry in your throat and nothing comes out. Stardark tosses his head restlessly, and you pat him soothingly.

The catapults are lined up one by one, to lay the great siege that will either free your family or plunge both armies into a war that could last months. You feel a great sadness creep over you as you watch.

"So this is what it means to be a ruler," you

whisper, as the armies ready to clash. Never have you felt so alone in your life, even as you know you have done all that your mother and father would have wanted you to.

THE END

PATHWAY 47

"I'm sorry, Tyrone, but I can't go underground. Show me where I may spend the night, and I will leave in the morning, to run the race as best I can."

Tyrone's face creases in anger, and his eyes flash, even in the dark. "I gave the word of an elf and a prince! I will aid you, but you must let me help you."

Wearily, you shrug his hand off your shoulder, the elfin enchantment gone. "I am a mortal, and I can only do what I can do. Tunnels and goblins aren't for me." You shudder at the thought.

Tyrone gets to his feet angrily. "I am trying to help!"

"And I am thanking you, but saying no."

The elf prince leaves in a flash of light, and you stagger to your feet. You are tired, tired, more tired in body and soul than you ever thought possible. Oh, how could you have danced this entire night as though nothing important but love and music were on your mind?

As you look up, Evelynne stands frowning in front of you. She has been giving you evil glances all night, and you guess that she and Tyrone must have had an understanding.

You say to her, "Is there a place I can rest? I need to sleep, for I'm leaving in the morning."

Evelynne brightens, and you know she is pleased that her rival is going. She inclines her head and says, "Follow me, then."

You weave after her, your head pounding and your feet like lead. She takes you not to one of the spiral buildings, but to a knoll with a wide-open door. You can hear faint sounds from within as she points. "In there, and you may rest."

"Thank you," you answer quietly, and you lurch inside, to see a great hall, lit up, with elves talking and gaming and drinking. Tyrone turns in great surprise as the doors begin to swing shut behind you.

"No!" he shouts. "No, Sarah, not in here!"

Too late, as the doors close with a great *boom*!

Tyrone's expression is one of great sadness as he comes to take your hand.

"What's happened?"

"You have entered the Elf Hill . . . where one night is as a hundred years to a mortal."

"And in the morning?"

"In the morning you may go home . . . to whatever home you will have a hundred years from now."

The elf holds you tightly as the tears begin to flow. You have been trapped, unwittingly, by a jealous elf.

THIS IS THE END OF YOUR ADVENTURE.

PATHWAY 48

You swallow and say, "I must ride on and fulfill my pledge. But if you can call your men together, in case I fail . . ."

"It will be done!"

The day fades into night and the night grows still about you, as riders gather and leave the encampment and drums send their muffled voices across the Elash, and you are lulled into sleep by the fireside, after eating a hot and spicy meal you can't name, but are unashamed to lick off your fingers afterward.

In the morning, the camp is deserted, but Stardark is tethered by your form, his eyes bright, as he nuzzles you awake.

You mount him stiffly, every little bruise and twinge like ice and fire in your legs. "Oh!" You muffle a gasp as you sit down, thinking it is no wonder that the scouts for your father are all grizzled and rawhide, if they have to sit in a saddle all day. You shake your dress out. "Poor rag! But when I make it home, I shall save enough of you to make a pillow out of, to remind me of this always." Even as you say it, it strikes you that you hope these memories will be of triumph.

Stardark nickers and shakes his head, his thick ebony mane dancing upon his neck. He is eager and ready to go, and so you give him his head, riding toward the horizon Garon pointed out to you last night as the direction of the Garden of Galatea.

It is nearly midday, and the hot wind has blasted your tender face, and the sun has soaked your hair and dress, and Stardark's black skin glistens with sweat and lather, when you pull up on the ridge that marks the edge of the Elash and look down into a verdant valley, a land so green you can almost drink it.

The fragrance of flowers and herbs drifts across the seering breeze, and you inhale deeply. But Stardark seems alert, as he lifts his neck, his crest arched, and he dances impatiently.

"Is it water you smell? Or what?" you ask, as you pat him, thinking of the warning that a dragon lies curled in the Garden. You urge him down into the valley, as mountain shadows fall across it—the Dynas Mountains, which you might have crossed another way, if you had not been so wary of the elves.

As you approach the Garden itself, centered in the tiny wall, walled by ancient gray stones, you see the glistening emerald form stretched out, and as you pull Stardark to a halt, the beast raises its head and looks in your direction.

The dragon is awake and awaiting you. You

freeze in the saddle, for though you are still too far away to really see the gleaming amber eyes and have them work their dragon magic on you, you're not too far away to be scared stiff. Claws like rapiers and wings as thin as tissue stretch as the reptile gets to its feet.

Stardark paws the ground nervously as he senses the ancient enemy of the skies. You stroke his neck comfortingly.

You have but two choices now: to ride off and sneak back, hoping to surprise the dragon later, or to charge in now and face whatever destiny offers you.

1. *If you ride into the Garden, dragon and all, turn to Pathway 27 (page 112).*

2. *But if you pretend to leave, hide, and then return, see Pathway 36 (page 140).*

About the Author

RHONDI VILOTT first got hooked on writing in third grade and spent most of her school years working on the school newspaper and in creative writing. She first began working on fantasy and science fiction in the 1970s, and attended the Clarion SF Writer's Workshop in 1979.

Although she has written romances for teens and adults, science fiction is her first love. And, although most writers claim poetic license, Rhondi likes to think she has a pilot's license—for flights of fantasy.

Rhondi lives with her husband, Howard, and their four children in California, and warns all her children's friends that anything they say may be used in a book about them.

Great Science Fiction by Robert Adams from SIGNET

(0451)
- ☐ THE COMING OF THE HORSECLANS (Horseclans #1) (131428—$2.75)*
- ☐ SWORDS OF THE HORSECLANS (Horseclans #2) (099885—$2.50)*
- ☐ REVENGE OF THE HORSECLANS (Horseclans #3) (133064—$2.95)*
- ☐ A CAT OF SILVERY HUE (Horseclans #4) (133056—$2.95)*
- ☐ THE SAVAGE MOUNTAINS (Horseclans #5) (129342—$2.95)*
- ☐ THE PATRIMONY (Horseclans #6) (133005—$2.95)*
- ☐ HORSECLANS ODYSSEY (Horseclans #7) (129350—$2.95)*
- ☐ THE DEATH OF A LEGEND (Horseclans #8) (129350—$2.95)*
- ☐ THE WITCH GODDESS (Horseclans #9) (117921—$2.50)*
- ☐ BILI THE AXE (Horseclans #10) (129288—$2.95)*
- ☐ CHAMPION OF THE LAST BATTLE (Horseclans #11) (133048—$2.95)*
- ☐ A WOMAN OF THE HORSECLANS (Horseclans #12) (125754—$2.50)*
- ☐ CASTAWAYS IN TIME (126645—$2.75)*

*Prices slightly higher in Canada

Buy them at your local bookstore or use coupon on last page for ordering.

Great Science Fiction from SIGNET

(0451)

- [ ] INTERGALACTIC EMPIRES: Isaac Asimov's Wonderful Worlds of Science Fiction #1 edited by Isaac Asimov, Martin H. Greenberg and Charles G. Waugh. (126246—$2.95)*
- [ ] THE SCIENCE FICTIONAL OLYMPICS: Isaac Asimov's Wonderful World of Science Fiction #2 edited by Isaac Asimov, Martin H. Greenberg and Charles G. Waugh. (129768—$3.50)*
- [ ] SUPERMEN: Isaac Asimov's Wonderful World of Science Fiction #3 edited by Isaac Asimov, Martin H. Greenberg and Charles G. Waugh. (132017—$3.50)*
- [ ] WIZARDS: Isaac Asimov's Magical Worlds of Fantasy #1 edited by Isaac Asimov, Martin H. Greenberg and Charles G. Waugh. (125428—$3.50)*
- [ ] WITCHES: Isaac Asimov's Magical Worlds of Fantasy #2 edited by Isaac Asimov, Martin H. Greenberg and Charles G. Waugh. (128826—$3.50)*
- [ ] COSMIC KNIGHTS: Isaac Asimov's Magical Worlds of Fantasy #3 edited by Isaac Asimov, Martin H. Greenberg and Charles G. Waugh. (133420—$3.95)*
- [ ] THE SLEEPING DRAGON: Guardians of the Flame #1 by Joel Rosenberg. (125746—$2.95)*
- [ ] THE SWORD AND THE CHAIN: Guardians of the Flame #2 by Joel Rosenberg. (128834—$2.95)*
- [ ] TIES OF BLOOD AND SILVER by Joel Rosenberg. (131673—$2.75)*

*Prices slightly higher in Canada.

Buy them at your local bookstore or use coupon on next page for ordering.

SIGNET Science Fiction You'll Enjoy

(0451)

- [ ] THE HAND OF GANZ by Isidore Haiblum. (133412—$2.75)*
- [ ] THE IDENTITY PLUNDERERS by Isidore Haiblum. (128265—$2.50)*
- [ ] JEHAD by Nicholas Yermakov. (126882—$2.75)*
- [ ] A RUMOR OF ANGELS by M. B. Kellogg. (123484—$2.50)*
- [ ] DANCER'S ILLUSION by Ann Maxwell. (124618—$2.50)*
- [ ] DANCER'S LUCK by Ann Maxwell. (122534—$2.50)*
- [ ] FIRE DANCER by Ann Maxwell. (119398—$2.50)*
- [ ] DRIFTGLASS by Samuel R. Delaney. (120922—$2.95)
- [ ] GOLD STAR by Zach Hughes. (126254—$2.25)*
- [ ] OUTCASTS OF HEAVEN BELT by Joan D. Vinge. (116534—$2.50)*

*Prices slightly higher in Canada

Buy them at your local bookstore or use this convenient coupon for ordering.

NEW AMERICAN LIBRARY,
P.O. Box 999, Bergenfield, New Jersey 07621

Please send me the books I have checked above. I am enclosing $_____
(please add $1.00 to this order to cover postage and handling). Send check or money order—no cash or C.O.D.'s. Prices and numbers are subject to change without notice.

Name _____

Address _____

City _____ State _____ Zip Code _____

Allow 4-6 weeks for delivery.
This offer is subject to withdrawal without notice.